Tales
from the
Pit

A series of short stories about playing in orchestra pits, dedicated to everyone who has ever played in one.

by Peter Neville

Cover illustration by Joan M. Jeans

Tales from the Pit

Peter Neville © 2003

Cover illustration: Joan M. Jeans © 2003

ISBN 1 903607 31 0

Typesetting and publication by:
Able Publishing
13 Station Road
Knebworth
Hertfordshire
SG3 6AP

www.ablepublishing.co.uk
email: fp@ablepublishing.co.uk

Tel: 01438 812320 / 814316
Fax: 01438 815232

Contents

All places and characters are fictional.

Foreword

by Margaret Grove

As someone who has been stage-struck since the age of three, I warmly recommend these *Tales*.

Whether in a grand opera house or in far humbler surroundings, the magic of theatre prevails.

The atmosphere is caught beautifully through the characters in the stories, and we smile in recognition.

M. G.

Margaret Grove was subprincipal first violin with D'Oyly Carte Opera Company, and has in her lifetime played in a wide variety of orchestra pits ranging from London's Sadlers Wells and other great theatres to village halls.

Author's Introduction

Welcome to that very special place, the orchestra pit.

The orchestra pit is a unique half-world, wherein the performers are not actors yet are on show, they have no overt discretion yet directly create emotion and atmosphere, and they are classically trained yet adapt to the idiom of the stage show.

The complete for-hire pit orchestra is now practically extinct. Now, an amateur operatic company planning its next show will appoint a Musical Director, who in turn will recruit his band one by one, through personal knowledge and recommendation. The band, assembled in this way from the local pool of jobbing musicians, will be a mixture of music teachers, shop assistants, and international lawyers who need the money. On the odd evening when one of them can't attend, he, or equally likely she, will send someone to deputise for them, expecting their dep to be able to play successfully through the show at sight.

The audience for an amateur operatic production has come to see a story told on the stage, not to admire musicians as in a formal orchestral concert. The musicians know this of course, but paradoxically it becomes all the more rewarding for them if they can place a musical phrase exactly to suit the action, or linger over a melody precisely the right amount to heighten the sentiment on stage.

Competent technicians they all are, yet they too have their worries, their feelings and their weaknesses. If these were recounted factually, nobody would believe it.

Hence these *Tales*.

Tales from the Pit

The New Girl

She stood uncertainly in the theatre staff car park on this dull Sunday morning, her brightly coloured coat and white cello case incongruous in these dingy surroundings. She didn't know how she could get in, with her cello, past a theatrical-scenery-delivery lorry which had backed hard up to the only obvious door. It was the last straw, considering she never really wanted to be here in the first place.

She recalled how her landlady had made her promise to spend every night in the house rather than let it be empty. Her landlady being a difficult person, she felt honoured to be so trusted, but it soon went sour. Only a few days after her landlady had departed to visit family in Canada, the local weekly amateur symphony orchestra in which they were both cellists was invited to participate in the Anglesey Festival, another orchestra having dropped out at the last minute. She wished she could have joined them; it was small consolation that her landlady would be equally disappointed when she came back and heard about it.

So, when that stranger phoned asking for her landlady, she let herself be talked into accepting this job herself. She wished she hadn't; theatrical music was sure to be too light-weight for her taste, although she didn't suppose that playing it would present any difficulty. And now, when she failed to turn up to the venue, the stranger would think she'd backed out, when she simply couldn't find where to go.

His arthritic joints protested as he manhandled his double bass out of his practice room into his hallway. He then cut himself on the zip of the bag in which he was packing it. He bumped his knee carrying it out through the doorway and, when he slid the bass into his car, he hit his head on the tailgate. Breathless from the exertion, he decided he was really too old for this sort of thing. He hadn't played for a while, so his fingertips would have gone soft and would be agony by the end of the week. He'd been meaning to sell his bass and had only agreed to do this week of *Merry Widow* as a special favour to the Musical Director. And as for the Katisha-like cellist whom the MD usually picked to sit next to him ...

As they simultaneously spotted each other, they both felt relieved: he, because this young girl was not Katisha; and she, because he radiated experience and knowledge.

"Oh, really! They should have told you," he exclaimed, "you couldn't have guessed to go in here by the dustbins. And now there's six doors and four staircases before you get to the pit. Except today, being the band call, I expect we're in the studio room. Just follow me."

In the studio room, the company were trying on costumes, stepping out dance routines, and giving no impression of having been rehearsing, as she supposed, six months for this moment. Along one side of the room, music stands and chairs had been set out, and she moved to the right of the conductor, as she would in a symphony orchestra.

"Where do I sit in the section?" she asked innocently.

"You *are* the section," smiled the bass, "and you'll be behind the violins, not facing them, don't ask me why but that's usually how it is. Oh, and don't call him the conductor, he's the Musical Director." He still remembered his own surprise on making these discoveries, thirty-five years and two hundred shows ago.

The MD came in at this moment and shook hands with the two musicians. He paused momentarily as he could not recognise the girl, and then answered her unspoken questions.

"Yes, it's me that phoned your landlady and got you instead. Well, what's the problem, a cellist is a cellist is a cellist, surely? And it's a lavish production – we've got *three* first violins and two seconds, *and* a harp."

"What are these then?" asked the cellist, having observantly spotted some band parts piled by the MD's rostrum and not placed out on the music stands.

"Ah, see for yourself," replied the MD, "they're the instruments we're missing out – a bassoon, a second trombone, er, yes … you two on the bass clef, we're really depending on you!"

She sneaked a quick look at the MD's score, and saw that it was a piano reduction. But she also saw on the score that occasional instrument names were written in, so she realised the MD might still always know which player had made any mistake.

She went to her music stand, of a strange design she'd never seen before with built-in light, and opened her part, her first sight of the music that would be performed to the paying public the day after tomorrow. She gave a horrified squeal. The music was handwritten and smudgily photo-reproduced. Apart from at the opening of each number, there were no clefs or key signatures at the beginning of the lines. She resented this discourtesy because the key seemed to change every couple of lines – into some horrendous keys – and all three cello clefs were in use. And even if she could read the music, she couldn't play it at sight, no way.

"Don't worry," said the bass player. "There are only three rules: be punctual, and you obviously are; don't contradict the MD; and always bring a flask. Meanwhile, have a swig from mine."

While she was studying her part, the remaining musicians had been assembling and making ready.

"Overture, please, beaten in one," commanded the MD. A torrent of self-confident music immediately rang round the room. The company applauded. But she, having got lost immediately, hadn't played a note. She wanted to hide in shame.

"Number one, company please, Pontevedro in Paree," said the MD next. The company put down the costumes to which they were making last-minute adjustments. Somebody, intently spray-painting shoes, missed the announcement and shame-facedly stopped when tapped by a fellow actor.

The cellist followed the beat like a hawk, playing just one note a bar, anything to try and keep up. The singing of the company did not distract her, as she had often played in orchestras accompanying choirs. A couple of more straightforward numbers followed. Soon, she was managing to hang on for a while before dropping out, with the double bass whispering occasional bar numbers to her when she seemed uncertain.

If this had been her amateur orchestra, the conductor would have stopped and gone over passages again, to identify mistakes or omissions or to improve the phrasing or balance. But this MD never stopped. Not until no.14a, which was a cello solo which she expounded in the wrong key. The MD stopped and, without saying a word, restarted. She had meanwhile spotted her error and was grateful for his tact.

At the end, she wondered how there could ever be a show in the tuneless cacophony they had just played. As she was about to pack away her cello, the viola player came up to her.

"Can I try your cello?" he asked. "I make violas, so I'm interested. I can't actually play the cello but I can probably get a sound out of it. Hm, very distinctive scroll, looks like the work of Cuthbert Brown. Have you had this valued? Could be worth the price of a very classy new car, you know. Oh, you got it from a distant cousin? What, just on condition you played it? Lucky you! OK, let's have a go."

At the viola player's first touch, the cello burst forth with a golden sound that crashed round the rehearsal room. The company all looked up in surprise. The cello's owner was ashamed at her ineffectual scratchings on what she had dismissed as a cast-off orange-box.

The next evening, having found her way into the theatre, she saw an attendance list to tick, with a pencil for the purpose hanging by a string from a hook on the wall. To her surprise, even the orchestra was listed and, yes, there, for real, was her very own name.

Asking the way through corridors designed for getting lost, she ended up in a low-ceilinged hall where an actor on a high chair under a glaring spotlight was being made up. She was about to back out when somebody shouted to her, "Through the curtain, dearie." The curtain turned out to be concealing a low headroom opening heavily scuffed around the edges.

Stumbling through, she found she was now in the orchestra pit, and she was the first in. Tripping over a tangle of wires and knocking a music stand over, she eventually found the stand carrying the cello part, in this unfamiliar location behind the violins and next to the double bass. Her music stand light was on, and the untidy mess of cables and adapters was all there just for the lights in the stands. She guessed that a carelessly planted cello spike in this heap of wiring could cause chaos in the electrics.

More relaxed now that she had safely arrived at her place, she looked up and around in wonderment, at the ceiling so far above, at the ornate proscenium arch, at the empty and silent but strangely expectant auditorium. If the true centre of the theatre was anywhere, it was here, the pit.

While it was the dress rehearsal for the actors and stage staff, the orchestra and even the MD were casually dressed and the auditorium remained fully lit. By immense concentration, she kept her place for almost the whole of the overture, even observing most of the key changes. The curtain opened, and the opening chorus started at once taking her by surprise. As she floundered around trying to catch up, a photographer leapt out of nowhere and, standing directly by her, took numerous flash photographs of the action on stage.

Hopelessly lost following this distraction, she sighed and turned the pages to the next number. This started well, until a voice behind her shouted, "Did you get your visuals?" With this surprise, she was again lost, and without the luxury of other cellists to follow. But this time, she would fight her way back. She fastened on to the next tempo change in her part, and waited, watching the MD like a hawk … this must be the moment …

Yes, she had climbed back on board. This music would not defeat her. But there were no warm slushy numbers as she expected, and even the famous tunes sounded harsh and crude. The actors struck her as wooden and uncertain. It was a scandal to be charging an audience good money to see this travesty of a show tomorrow.

On opening night, a fleet of minibuses from the local Old Folks' Home was drawn up at the side of the theatre, with staff carefully easing their charges into wheelchairs, unloading them via the minibus tail-lifts, and wheeling them patiently into the theatre. Although the cellist could not imagine ever becoming that age, she did guess that these old folks had probably been looking forward to this show for a long time. She really must do her best for them.

Dressed in concert black, she took her seat in the pit, tuned up, opened her part and sat ready. The bass player showed her how to adjust the light. He marvelled at the heavily shaded setting she preferred. Oh, to have such youthful sharp eyes again.

But she was in no joys-of-youth mood. Though the auditorium had been empty yesterday, she had already felt its atmosphere weighing on her. Now that the auditorium had filled and was alive with chatter, she felt too close to the audience, who were on the same level as her, just three feet away and separated by only a low curtained rail.

The auditorium lights started to dim. The MD, resplendent in white tie and tails, made a grand entrance under a spotlight. The chatter died away. She felt more naked than on any concert platform. What did she think she was doing here? As the house lights continued to fade, her universe shrank to just the music in front of her and the MD's baton illuminated by the spotlight. Why had she ever agreed to this? She was now inescapably and very publicly responsible for producing the entire cello line all by herself. She'd never done anything remotely like this before. The downbeat ...

When she staggered home at the end, she was so exhausted she could remember nothing, except that she had a rather effective arpeggiated pizzicato passage in no.2; it would be fun to do that tomorrow, even if the rest was noisy and unmemorable.

As the week went on, she began to piece together the plot, harder to do from the pit than from the auditorium. Although the story was cleverly constructed, the ending jarred. The Merry Widow tells the ambassador that he would do the fatherland no service by marrying her, because on re-marriage she forfeits the money which the fatherland needs to retain, yet a moment later she reveals that the money would have stayed with the fatherland after all because it goes to her new husband. And then Danilo, who has throughout tried to avoid being considered a fortune-hunter, says he would have married her if she had been twice as rich.

Nonetheless, she began to enjoy the show more. The next night, she noticed she had a lovely duet with the flute in no.7, and each following night, she had to admit to herself that more of the numbers were revealing themselves as gems. And each night, more and more of the awkward musical passages were falling into place.

She began to notice that she had several solos, all in Act 2. She wasn't nervous at all, perhaps because the realisation had only slowly crept up on her. It was the two gasps every night at the same points in her solo in no.14a that puzzled her.

"I'm not playing *so* badly, am I?" she asked the bass.

The next night, he gave her the answer: "It's because of on-stage. No, don't glance up while you're playing, you'll only get distracted. They have a special curtain and they change the lighting so that suddenly you see two figures dancing behind it. Then you see that it's Camille and Valencienne, and then they separate. So it's telling you that their romance is doomed. It's a jolly effective piece of staging, I've not seen it done before. And to cap it all, your solo is a reprise of their opening duet, I expect you'd noticed. Talk about milking the sentiment, no wonder the old dears gasp."

She enjoyed Friday's performance. She knew her way round the music now. She could spare enough of her ear to notice her friend on the double bass with his effectively rumbustious passage in no.12 'Women, women, women.' A moment later, she had an answering solo, a cleverly distorted version of the 'You'll find me at Maxim's' theme, which told the audience, more directly than any words, that Danilo was sick of his empty womanising life. This was more conversational even than chamber music. She knew she really mattered, was part of the drama, especially in no.14a, where the MD, sensing her growing confidence, would hold the orchestra back and let *her* shape the melody.

His indulgence didn't extend to an awkward recitative in no.17, where she could never quite read his beat, but the other strings would always hold on and wait for her. Now she knew what teamwork really meant.

During the second interval on that Friday night, a lady in the audience came up to the pit rail to complain to the double bass that he was standing in her line of sight. The cellist knew she should keep her head down and take no part in this, but, feeling she owed the double bass some moral support after all his help, she turned round. The cellist recognised the complainant as having been one of her school teachers from some years back, and interrupted the tirade to introduce herself.

"Oh, I am pleased you spoke," replied her ex-teacher. "I'm so glad to see you here. What a distinction for you, to be playing in this fine band! I always hoped you'd achieve something but I never quite knew if you would." With that, she returned to her seat, leaving the double bass in peace.

The Saturday matinée started with two toddlers at opposite corners of the auditorium performing an antiphonal chorus of wailing, to the accompaniment of rustling of sweets *fortissimo*, with loud commentary from a pair of old ladies.

By the end of Act 1, one toddler had been taken out, all sweets had been eaten, and the ladies were asleep. As Act 2 began, the cellist was totally relaxed and decided to play for herself and her fellow musicians, if the audience were going to be so unappreciative. When she started her first solo, her cello seemed to come alive. She was no longer consciously playing it; it was doing the playing for her. She and her cello had become an indivisible unit. The distinctive mellow yet transparent Cuthbert Brown sound which she had at last unlocked billowed round the theatre. The violins and viola looked round incredulously.

And so it was for her remaining Act 2 solos, all effortlessly wonderful, with that elusive combination of accuracy, beauty and authority. In particular during no.14a, she was convinced she could sense sniffling into lavender-scented handkerchiefs.

When the lights rose at the interval, the double bass player briefly said, "You'll do." She had hoped that, as her guide and mentor, he might have been more demonstrative, perhaps pat her.

He was in fact so delighted he would have lifted her up and hugged her, if he had dared.

For the Saturday evening, everyone was so concerned to get everything right that the performance had a bottle-tight stiffness; the spontaneity had gone. Her solos were competent but not inspired, and so it was for everyone

"Do all shows peak out at the Saturday matinée?" she asked the bass as she packed her cello at the end.

"No, it's live theatre, you can never predict. Sometimes Thursday's the best night, and people get overconfident and don't concentrate on the Friday. Or else sometimes it only really comes good on the Saturday night. Or sometimes it just never quite gels. Anyway, good luck, and all the best."

She felt cold air wafting into the pit, and replied, "Bye, and thanks for all your help."

Her parents came to visit her on the Sunday, and she enjoyed describing her week to them. She completely forgot to tell them about missing the Anglesey Festival.

Then it hit her. Back at the office on Monday, she still had the tunes going round her head, but now without the pleasurable anticipation of re-creating those tunes and winning that emotional sigh from the paying public. She moped her way through the morning, in no mood to join her colleagues for their pub lunch. While eating her yoghurt, she leafed idly through a free magazine that had been thrust at her on the way in. There was an article with a telephone number to ring, about a new film studio that was looking for secretaries, seamstresses, wig-makers ...

Perhaps, she thought, they might also need musicians. She rang the number.

The Bagpiper

The Hon. Secretary of the district Caledonian Association sighed inwardly. He had been asked to recommend a bagpiper for the local operatic society's forthcoming production of *Brigadoon*. He was quite often asked to recommend bagpipers for weddings and Burns Nights, but for an operatic production? He would have suggested Hamish or Andrew, but Hamish had a contract on an oil-rig and Andrew wanted to be free to dash up and visit his sick mother in Scotland.

He wondered about asking his Chairman. The Secretary knew his Chairman to be a very fine piper, in truth better than both Hamish and Andrew, but the Chairman did also happen to be heir to one of the great Scottish dukedoms. The estates which he would one day own were measured not in acres but in hundreds of square miles. You couldn't ask such a man to play for a local amateur group for pocket money. Or could you?

The Chairman had come to divide his time between Scotland, assisting his father with his heavy social obligations, and Mayfair, working for a respected art dealership. He did the latter neither as a hobby nor because he needed the money, but in total earnest, in order to prove to the world (and to himself) that he was competent to earn his own living, regardless of whose son he was. That is why he readily agreed to be the bagpiper for the production of *Brigadoon*.

"No, kindly don't improvise, just play what's written,"

the Musical Director commented in his unflappable but firm Welsh voice. The bagpiper's temper flared and he was about to lecture the MD on the art of piping and to list the many cups and medals he had won as a piper, when, fortunately, he was struck by the humour of a musical with a Scottish locale performed in England under Welsh musical direction. The few seconds this took were enough for him to suppress his anger and to come to the realisation that, in this world, he was not the influential figure that he was outside – here, he was just the hired technician and it was the MD who was in command.

"Yes, I'm sorry, I understand," he replied to the MD.

But already the MD had dismissed the incident and was calling "Orchestra – number twenty-six please, Fiona and Tommy, your song 'From this day on'."

At the end of this Sunday run-through of the music before the week's run, the producer called the bagpiper aside to explain to him when to enter on-stage and where to stand; the bagpiper was needed only in the second act, and then only twice. The bagpiper had no difficulty following these directions during the production, nor in playing the music from memory as he had to, but, while he took pride in doing his specialist job well, he could not get as excited about appearing on stage as did the members of the company.

He was impressed by the accuracy of the Highland accent in which the company's elocutionist had drilled them – Scotsmen usually shudder at English efforts to copy the accent; even if passable, it's often from the wrong part of Scotland. On the other hand, he was contemptuous of the crudity of the devices which he saw in use backstage for creating effects, such as the exaggerated make-up and the vegetable-oil smoke burner for generating "mist."

The plot, so far as he could gather what it was from backstage, struck him as inane. The Highland village of Brigadoon existed only one day in every hundred years? It was a love story between a villager and an outsider? People paid money to see such rubbish?

One afternoon during the week, the receptionist at the art dealership brought him a fax. It was what he had been fearing but had hoped might yet be averted – one of their best clients had decided to sue over a disputed valuation he had given. The partners called him in. The meeting was sticky and unpleasant. 5pm came and went, 6pm, 7pm ...

The partners urged him to close the matter by giving in, but he refused because he would lose all credibility in the art world. At length he simply rose and walked out of the meeting, the problem unresolved. He rushed home, changed straight into his Highland gear and, without stopping to eat, drove to the theatre. In the theatre, time has its own unreal speed, and he had no idea at what time o'clock he was due on-stage.

As he turned his car into the theatre car-park, he found to his dismay that it was full. Until tonight, he had always arrived, in common with the other performers, well before the performance started, when there was plenty of space. He was resigning himself to a time-consuming search for kerbside parking when he noticed a car leaving. As it drew level, he recognised the driver as the make-up artist.

She wound down her window and shouted cheerfully across to him, "Hello dear, I've done my bit for them tonight, now it's over to you! *And* you can have my parking space."

It was the first friendly voice he had heard in hours. She'd said nothing about him being late; that was a good sign.

He reached the stage door and cursed himself for not having memorised the security number for the door. It was no use doing as he usually did, waiting for other performers to arrive and let him in; they had all arrived hours ago. Nor was it any use knocking; none of the dressing rooms was within earshot. He would have to use the front entrance.

On reaching it, he saw the foyer staff gathering up used cups and glasses, from which he deduced that the interval had just finished. He expected to be challenged, a bagpiper walking in in full Highland dress at this time in the evening, but he was ignored until he put his ear to the auditorium door.

"Changed your entrance, have they?" asked an attendant matter-of-factly.

"Yes, that's right," he replied with relief.

He had indeed cut it fine. He very soon recognised the music of the tipsy wedding dance, at the end of which he was meant to stand on-stage to play his totally contrasting dirge. The dirge was also the music for a solo funeral dance around Harry's lifeless body.

Not wishing to leave an empty silence, nor indeed wishing to worry the company, who would soon be frantically looking for him in the wings, he opted to make a premature rather than a belated entrance. Bravely playing, he burst into the darkened auditorium during the tipsy dance and walked forwards towards the stage.

The look on the actors' faces was a picture of total bewilderment and astonishment. The orchestra raggedly stopped playing and the solo funeral dance proceeded. At the end of the funeral dance, he wished the floor could swallow him up, because there was no way on to the stage; there, a little later, he would have to play his other number, a short mood-setting piece covering the last scene-change of the musical, from noisy bustling New York to misty romantic Scotland.

So he did the only possible thing – he walked down the

few steps into the orchestra pit and out of sight. He was instantly fascinated by the musicians'-eye view of the production; they were so close to the stage it felt almost as much part of the action as being on-stage. The musicians must have worked out their places in the pit carefully, as they had difficulty in making space for him to sit on the floor. But they didn't question his right to be there, and that made him feel proud.

From down there, he saw the effect produced by all those crude devices which he had held in such contempt. As the heroine slowly slipped out of the hero's grasp, supposedly to vanish for 100 years, under dimming lights and a pall of misty smoke, with a musical accompaniment that was being produced live all around him, he was amazed at the power of the illusion. The couple were absurdly ill-matched, a sophisticated twentieth-century American and a simple eighteenth-century Highland lass, but he still felt a lump in his throat for them. So *that* was the lure of the stage.

To save trouble, he decided to play his second number while remaining in the pit, and this worked out well. At the end of the show, he made towards the MD to apologise for the earlier contretemps, but the MD held him by the shoulder and said, "No, wait, I was over-ruled but you've proved I was right. Look, see the script for yourself -

'..*as many of the townsmen are now a little tipsy, the wedding dance is done in that spirit. The dance stops abruptly and all start back in horror as the sound of bagpipes is heard, beginning the lament.*'

- I *told* the producer, you're *meant* to interrupt the dance and shock everybody. Well, you did that tonight all right. Just do it every night, something different so they always look genuinely surprised – I'll square it with the producer."

This was a challenge he enjoyed. Each night he would

outwit and surprise the tipsy-dancers, often using the orchestra pit as his refuge. There, the aromas of the pit were an unexpected novelty to him: the bitter sharp smell of the hot dust on the illuminated music-stands, the sickly-sweet glue binding of the band parts, the oil used by the trombonist, the rosin used by the string players ...

But what really impressed him were the musicians, showing such obvious pleasure in their work. To avoid being a nuisance, he would sit by a different musician each night. Seeing him, each of them would turn gloomily to some page or other of their band part and point out where it always went wrong for them, or where they lost the place, or where it went adrift from the singers. And each time he could notice nothing untoward, so high were their standards. It would be marvellous, he thought, if he could ever become one of them.

The week flew by. But he did not omit to keep in daily touch with Scotland by phone.

"Oh, hello Morag," he said cheerfully as he recognised his father's secretary answering on the Friday, "can I speak to my father please? I'm having a super time this week, it's marvellous, I never thought I would enjoy it so much."

"Yes, I know," said Morag, "you've said so every day. I'm very pleased to hear you so happy. I can't, er, put you through to your father just this minute, but I know your mother wants to speak to you. Here she is."

"Oh, mother!" he babbled excitedly. "This has opened a new window for me. I never knew what the theatre was really like from the inside. I want to take it up. On the musical side, perhaps. Learn an orchestral instrument ..."

"Yes, dear," his mother interrupted. "How long does your present engagement continue? Ah, just until tomorrow night? Well, listen dear, your father can't talk to you at the moment, but we're all delighted you've had a chance to participate in something that's obviously so fulfilling for you. Why don't you phone again tomorrow, as soon as it's finished? Yes, of course I'll wait up."

It was agreed that, for the Saturday night performance, he would revert to standing on-stage and not playing until the tipsy dance had finished. But that was an hour or two in the future. From the first note of the overture, this performance had a crisp immediacy. This night, all the scenes were as strong and effective as could possibly be imagined.

For no reason that he could fathom, he found himself especially caught up in the second-act scene where Harry is found dead but, to spare his father's feelings, the latter is not told straight away. The music was no add-on tonight; the bagpiper could hear how it too was telling the story. The insistent doom-laden rhythm, and the mournful phrases one by one from various instruments in the band, added poignancy to the men's chorus. In a few moments, he would have to take his own turn to play Harry's funeral dirge, and he had better be good.

He walked across onto the stage with an air of dignified assurance which he did not feel, although his lifelong upbringing made it second-nature for him to put on that act. His manner also conveyed a hint of humility, which he did very much feel, with the display of such dedicated musical competence all round him. He gently inflated his bag, placed his fingers ready on the chanter and tensed his elbow against the bag.

He suddenly had the vivid and strange feeling that his father was present in spirit to encourage him.

His fingers danced over the chanter and the drones rang out harmoniously – the drones could go out of tune all too easily, giving the characteristic discord that made bagpipes so unpopular. But not this evening. He was accompanying the dancer as well as a dancer could ever wish, and he could sense that the dancer's performance was also her best ever.

As the sequence approached its end, he took a last breath to inflate the bag, estimating the amount that would leave the bag about one-quarter full at the end of the last note. But the exceptional quality of his playing had somehow gone to his head and made him breathe too freely. He misjudged, putting just too much air into the bag.

He realised his mistake at once, but there was nothing he could do about it. The mistake had no immediate effect but would become all too obvious at the end, after the dance. Then, the excess air would vent from the bag with a squawk resembling a brace of strangled grouse.

He played on, as he had to for the dancer's sake, but inwardly counting the seconds to that ignominious squawk that would undo all the magnificent impression he knew he was giving.

Because the company had become unfamiliar with the original stage layout being revived tonight, the pall-bearers had unwittingly put Harry's body a few inches out of place. The dancer could not dance round the body and draw the dead Harry's plaid over his face in the stipulated time; she found herself having to improvise two extra steps.

The bagpiper saw. Improvising music to fit a dance was second nature to him – had he not won cups and medals to prove it? Watching the dancer like a hawk, he added the two extra bars she needed. This exactly used up his excess air, so avoiding the squawk. And without his mistake, he would not have had enough air left to make the necessary improvisation. He could hardly credit his double luck. Was there really someone "up there" looking after him tonight?

As she moved across, downstage of the piper, to make her exit, the dancer touched him gently in thanks. The rest of the company, who sensed that they had been in the presence of extraordinary bagpipe playing, looked at him almost in awe.

His second number involved simply marching across the stage in front of the curtain while piping music to prepare the audience to "return" from New York to the Highlands. Doing this, he was spontaneously cheered. The stage, music-making, admiration and applause – what a potently addictive cocktail. He was hooked.

Directly after the show, having said his goodbyes, he rang his parents on his car phone.

"Morag!" he exclaimed, surprised to hear his father's secretary answer. "What are you doing, still in the castle at this hour?"

"Er, er, your Grace, er, here's your mother," Morag muttered.

Silly girl, what is the matter with her, he thought, it's my father who's 'your Grace,' not me. Then he addressed his mother: "Oh, mother, it was wonderful. I must do more of it. I'd no idea how it would bite me, making music for the theatre."

"Well, dear," his mother cut in, "you can't."

"What d'you mean, I can't?"

"Your father is, er, that is, he was taken very ill yesterday morning, and ..."

"Well, how is he now?"

"You impatient boy, now you force me to tell you. He, he died about an hour ago."

"Mother! Why – I've phoned every day like I always do – how *could* you not tell me ..."

"Well, we knew just how much you were enjoying this theatre thing, we wanted you to be able to complete your week in it. Because it was your last chance. You'll have to leave your art job too, of course. Normal life is over for you now. You're a public figure, or you will be tomorrow, when your father's death is in the newspapers."

In a daze, he disconnected the phone. So *that* was why, earlier, he had so strongly sensed his father's presence.

He knew he would come to miss his father but, to his shame, his very first reaction was how he would miss the theatre and could never repeat his magic week in Brigadoon.

The Cellist

The theatre was in a run-down Victorian shopping area. On this bright Sunday morning, the front entrance to the theatre was locked and barred. He could find no way in until, on his second walk round the block, he noticed an unmarked entrance set back round the corner between a seedy bookshop and a public lavatory. His guess was right: this was indeed the stage door. It had no handle and opened outwards only, but with a well-practised kick born of experience of many such doors, he managed to bounce it open.

Once inside, he could hear excited girls' voices and a percussionist tuning his timps. Following these sounds, he carried his cello down a flight of concrete steps and along a dingy winding corridor, until he came upon the rehearsal room. The morning sun hardly penetrated the dirt caking the skylight, only just enough to pick out a stagehand who was examining a pile of upright chairs with yellow foam padding oozing out through splits in the red plastic upholstery; the stagehand was selecting the least torn chairs for the band. Ah, the glamour of showbiz ...

He reflected on this scene. Though just in early middle age, he already felt his musical ability ebbing. Would he still be up to this job? Would his eyes recognise the notes on the page? Would his fingers respond? Would his bow create a good sound? Should he not, after all, concentrate on his 9-to-5 job in the council offices? He pulled himself together and introduced himself to the Musical Director for this production of *Carmen*; they exchanged the customary pleasantries.

With ample time before the orchestra was due to start, and still only a few instrumentalists there, the cellist walked to his place far left of the MD, sat down, took a gulp of coffee from his flask and opened the cello part, which was already on the music stand. The music stand looked old enough and battered enough to have seen service in the Boer War, and the locking screws for adjusting its height and angle were seized solid. He made a mental note to bring his pliers tomorrow.

The band part was written in faded purple manuscript on yellowing paper, with a familiar sickly-sweet pungence from the glue binding. The manuscript was in a scarcely legible hand, with the tails of the notes well spaced from the heads, the dots of dotted notes scattered far afield and the leger lines irregularly spaced and fatter than the noteheads. What was legible was almost obliterated by heavy pencilled annotations, many of which contradicted each other.

Eventually he deciphered enough to see that this was a much-revised version of Bizet's work. At the cellist's high point in the opera – the menacing pedal notes under Carmen's card-game song in which she foretells her death – the band part in this version stonily said "Tacet."

This disappointment aside, the band call went well enough to dispel his agonies of self-doubt, and he looked forward to the dress rehearsal on Monday evening.

When he found his way into the pit on the Monday, however, he was daunted by how cramped it was – it made his bachelor flat seem positively spacious. Whoever had set up the pit had no idea how much room string instruments need for bowing.

The cellist had been positioned next to the viola player, who was therefore a key individual in how congenial the cellist would find this week. The violist turned out to be a military type used to having his own way, and much irritated by the cellist's requests for more playing room. Nor was the violist disposed to pass the time by conversation when the dress rehearsal failed to start on time, even though there was little else to do, as the band sat and waited, instruments at the ready.

To make good use of this wait, the cellist decided to adjust his music stand. Wrenching at it with his pliers, he somehow blew the light bulb in it, and had to ask the MD to summon an electrician. In his embarrassment at being the cause of this further delay, he found himself misreading the beat, miscounting rests, playing in the wrong keys and forgetting accidentals.

Matters didn't improve during the week; his playing remained badly out of form. His cello seemed to pick up his mood, sticking and squeaking, especially whenever he had to play the mid-stave E♭; he remembered hearing other cellists complaining of this problem, but it had never happened to him. Also, his bow was playing up; he had a routine of changing to successively heavier grades of rosin as his strings habitually became stodgier during the course of the week, but it was so hot and humid in this pit that he was already on his heaviest rosin by Thursday and he still couldn't get his cello to respond properly.

It didn't help that he was out of sympathy with many aspects of the production. He cringed every night when they approached the duet in which Micaela, the prissily pure "girl from back home", pleads with Don José to return to her. What a mawkish bass line! **Doh,** *doh* **doh,** *doh* **reh,** *reh* **reh,** *reh* **mee**... Even the audience every night seemed embarrassed by this duet.

He didn't think such weak music would be Bizet's own writing, but he checked and it was.

In despair at his poor playing, he decided after the Friday to change to his second cello, a three-centuries-old Flemish instrument. Clumsily repaired in the past, it was now valueless, but he kept it for its soft sweet tone. He hardly ever played it in public.

On arriving in the pit, he tuned it up to the sharp pitch that prevails as the week goes on. The ancient cello creaked ominously in protest.

In the opening scene, he noticed for the first time that the duet where Micaela and Don José declare their love was an ingenious preview of the "cringe" duet where Micaela still declares her love but Don José spurns her. No sooner had he warmed to this discovery than one of the tuning pegs of his cello sprang loose, under the unaccustomed extra string tension of the sharp pitch.

During the subsequent dialogue, he laboriously retuned, whisper-quietly. All four strings needed further adjustment at least twice before stabilising in tune.

As the cello continued to creak and shudder dangerously, he reflected on his stupidity. At the end of his playing career, losing his touch, hardly called on to play any more, how silly to think that changing to this other cello could make any difference.

After a few numbers, the combination of the heat, string tension and heavy playing were taking their toll; his cello was developing nasty cracks. And all for nothing, as its contributions were drowned out in the full orchestral passages. He felt like packing up there and then, and walking out of the pit for ever. After the interval, he wished he had, when Micaela entered for her embarrassing scene. Oh no, **doh,** *doh* **doh,** *doh* **reh,** *reh* **reh,** *reh* **mee..*

But what was this? She had discarded her formal heavily embroidered dark jacket which she had worn all week, in favour of a simple open-necked white blouse. And her hair, all week primly tied in a tight bun, was combed out loose, rich and black, into its full glistening waist-length glory.

She had revealed herself as infinitely more desirable than Carmen.

Some instinct made him turn his cello towards her. He started to play his line with an intensity it didn't really merit. The rising bass line, **doh,** *doh* **doh,** *doh* **reh,** *reh* **reh,** *reh* **mee**, in the sweet and melting tone of his old cello blended as one into her pleading voice as the emotion poured out of her.

Urging his cello on to its limits and coaxing its most sympathetic tone from it, he matched, note for note, the rising despair of spurned love in her voice. Don José, in a brutally sudden different time signature, sang his answer of rejection. Again she pleaded. Again he rejected.

The brilliance of Bizet's writing was revealed as the cello line and Micaela's voice combined into a sound of almost painful beauty, the effect heightened by her captivating yet unaffected appearance. Only a saint or a madman could have rejected this overwhelming appeal. But Don José rejects her. The cellist had a strange feeling that it was himself, not Don José, who was performing the duet with Micaela. By the end of the duet, the cellist felt totally drained.

The duet did not receive the dutiful light clapping of the previous nights. There was, instead, a stunned silence. The audience understood for the first time the depth to which Carmen, in every way Micaela's inferior, must have corrupted Don José's soul. For everybody there that night, the opera had taken on a new meaning.

The cellist nursed his exhausted instrument through the rest of the performance and pondered the likely repair costs. The other bass instruments intuitively picked up his situation and put extra warmth into sustaining the bass line in support. Now he would *have* to give up. He had two cellos neither of which he could use, he was a passenger whom the other bass clef players were having to carry, and, worse still, he was getting carried away by a pretty girl who could sing a little.

At the final curtain, Micaela reaped a thunderous ovation. Even the band was applauded. The violist, to the cellist's astonishment, shook the latter's hand and said, "Well done, lad." At which the double bass player, who had, untypically and rather hurtfully, ignored the cellist all week, leaned forward and patted the cellist's shoulder, saying "Yes, good work, chum."

When the house lights rose, the cellist started to pack his cello in its case, all the while trying to put a disturbingly insistent vision of Micaela out of his mind. He knew that such emotions were absurd for him. He now saw that on all possible counts, he had reached the end of his playing career. As for his damaged cello, his best course of action was now blindingly obvious: he would not bother to have it repaired at all.

He rose to go, and could hear cheering from behind the curtain, followed immediately by the sound of the scenery being dismantled. Heavy-hearted as he left his last orchestra pit, he pushed his way into the under-stage passage and continued towards the now familiar flight of concrete steps up to the outside. A biting wind was blowing in through the open stage door. In the black night beyond, he could see dense flurries of rain lit by the stage-door lamp. A rivulet of rainwater was beginning to trickle in to the building, down the flight of concrete steps.

Wearily, he began to tread up the flight. As he was about to step out of the theatre for ever into the cold dark wetness, he felt someone tapping him on the back. Turning round carefully, so as not to hit the cello against the walls, not that it mattered now, the cellist saw a stagehand holding a note.

"You're to come to the cast party," said the stagehand.

"Don't be ridiculous," said the cellist. "Musicians *never* go to cast parties," and made to go.

"Well," insisted the stagehand, "you're to read this."

Gruffly, the cellist seized the proffered note, and saw that it was written in haste on the back of a good-luck card.

He read:

Dear Cellist,

Tonight I was going to give up the stage. I was getting typecast in this thankless rôle, at least it's thankless the way producers always want it done. So, on this my last night, with nothing left to lose, I did it my way, and at once I could hear you were with me. You understood. You were playing differently somehow, you were really supporting me.

You restored my dream that I can make a professional career on the stage.

But I can't do it by myself.

Wherever I perform, you must always come with me as my cellist. Please come to the cast party and take me home.

Yours, Micaela.

The Harpist

She inched her 12-year-old car forwards in the unexpected traffic queue approaching the bypass roundabout. She was not worried yet about the delay, as she had set off in plenty of time.

Harpists always did. It got them the best parking place to unload their instruments and, even more important, it gave them time to tune up on arrival. None of this casual adjustment of a single joint, which is all that woodwind players seemed to need, or even the violinists' quick corrections to just four strings, easily checked by playing adjacent strings together. No, she would have 47 strings to tune, each needing painstaking checking against octaves and fourths and fifths. And as her harp had got very hot at that civic reception earlier today, each *would* need to be tuned. Which reminded her, some of her tuning pegs would soon need repair – they weren't holding very well.

On eventually reaching the roundabout, she found everyone was being diverted off the bypass and through a hopelessly congested village. In the stop-start traffic, her car seemed to feel very hot, but at last, she regained the main road. She was still on schedule for the opening night of *Lilac Time*, a fanciful musical play with Schubert as the central character, using Schubert tunes.

Yesterday, the dress rehearsal had gone quite well for her, although the harp part had few places to shine. At least, it was practical to play, unlike her last show, some time ago, *Land of Smiles*, for which she felt she had needed twelve fingers on each hand.

As her car picked up speed, it suddenly coughed and stalled, and she was only just able to coast into a layby. The car had been her uncle's; he had given it to her for her eighteenth birthday four years ago, and it had been reliable until now. Perhaps it somehow knew that he had just died.

She gave up trying to restart her car. She reached for her mobile phone to call the breakdown service, but could not get a signal. She could just see a filling station ahead; she could phone from there. Dare she meanwhile leave her harp in the car? Then again, could she afford to wait for the breakdown service?

Of all her jobs, she so wanted to excel at *this* one. Her diary was well filled with playing in restaurants, art galleries, weddings and suchlike, but not with her great love, pit orchestras. Those opportunities were rare, and she wanted to prove that harps were indispensable in pits. This would not be easy, since at the *Lilac Time* band call the day before yesterday, she had noticed that the MD's score had listed the instruments of the band in descending order of necessity. There, named as the last, yes the very last, was "harp".

Yet this MD had still gone ahead and included her in this band. Arriving late and out of tune for the opening night was no way to repay his faith. Therefore she decided not to risk the wait for breakdown assistance.

She unloaded her harp, set it on her trolley and wheeled it to the filling station. She explained her plight to the cashier. He nodded, and made none of the usual jokes about harps and parties.

She watched the cars pulling in, particularly the big estate cars. She had thought of entering quizzes, naming "estate cars" as her specialist subject, until she realised that she would probably be beaten – by some other harpist.

Then a particular fine estate car rolled majestically in. It puzzled her, she couldn't recognise the model. Never mind, it seemed to have no passengers or luggage, it would do fine. As its driver emerged to fill up, she was delighted to see he was a bearded young man. Perfect. When he came in to pay, she approached him. She was very beautiful and knew it. In a few moments, she and her harp were on their way, in his car.

"Thanks for rescuing me," she said, "but I'm puzzled, I can't make out what car this is. Is it a new model? No, really?! That means it's the same age as *me!* And you do what? Take it to competitions? Where they judge its condition and cleanliness? Well, I'm sure you'll win, I've never seen anything to match this one."

She thought his hobby was mad, but kept her thoughts to herself. She returned to small talk, until they arrived at the theatre.

In trying to help her carry her harp down a flight of steps, against her protestations of self-sufficiency, he managed to topple it off its trolley. He was about to try to steady it by the large flat area of its coat, until she deftly slapped his hand away and, with the same arm movement, caught her harp by its frame.

Really, this man was a liability; he could easily have damaged the strings *and* the frame. Still, he had helped when she needed it, and she rewarded him with a hug that he was unlikely to forget in a hurry. He stammered his apology that he could not collect her at the end of the evening. Just as she was breathing a secret sigh of relief, he promised to visit the show later in the week.

She set up her harp in the pit in the conventional place, next to the cello and in front of the bass. The bass player, an old family friend, had already arrived, and readily agreed to return her to her abandoned car at the end of the evening and sort her out.

The MD, in evening trousers, T-shirt and cardigan, called in to the pit to check on any problems, and, seeing the harp, suggested she move to the other side of the pit.

"What, get deafened by the percussion and brass? Why?"

"Oh, never mind, it was just a thought. I'd better finish changing. See you later."

In her present position with the stage on her left, the harp would be between her and audience, and the bass player suggested to her that the MD's idea had been simply to make her sit facing the other way, showing her off better to the audience. Shrugging, she started to tune up. The carpeted floor of the pit was good for disguising mishaps such as dropped pencils, but she would have preferred a wooden floor, to give extra resonance to the harp.

The first-night audience, mostly pensioners, flocked in early. She conscientiously finished tuning, even though, with this nearly full house, the humidity and temperature were likely to rise and negate her efforts. At least she would be in tune with herself and would not be ashamed to be heard.

The MD, now formally dressed, sidled into the pit, checked that all of his band were there, and sat down to wait.

Soon, the house lights darkened. The opening of the overture borrowed the opening theme of Schubert's Unfinished Symphony. During her few bars' rest at the start, she was delighted to hear that this band was taking this sentimental musical seriously, and not playing carelessly or with embarrassment. It was an old-fashioned show, and she could sense that this old-fashioned audience were loving it.

Throughout the evening, she, too, played her part as she felt it deserved, but never felt she had made much impression, except for forty or so glissandi, which were all prominently audible. One or two glissandi would be acceptable, she thought, but 40 in one evening was bordering on vulgarity. Harps could do so much more ...

Returning home in the early hours, she collected a message off her voicemail. Her uncle's funeral was to be on Friday afternoon, and would she play the harp at it?

This meant she would have to send a dep to play the Friday

evening performance. Whom to send? Not her old teacher, he was sniffy about operatic playing, he would play woodenly yet with a technical mastery that would show her up. Her best friend from music college? No, she was also too good. Her pupil? No, not experienced enough.

Next day, she worked her way down her list of names, to find the most suitable ones were all already busy, not surprising at this short notice. Then she came to a possible, her own age and living in the next county; they had struck up a friendship at a harp summer school last year. Quite good, had performed a movement from the Boïeldieu concerto, and not likely to be a competitor for work in this particular county.

That settled, she could concentrate on the evening performance, in which she would identify the slushiest numbers, where she could add most to the sound picture and would, such was her aim, make shows without a harp simply unthinkable.

She dropped no.4 from her list of possibles. It had started well from her point of view, with a mushy accompaniment of plucked strings. Her sound cut through effortlessly, with a rich sonorous clarity. Really, pizzicato strings should be forbidden when there was a harp around. But then she sensed, from audience laughter, that the number then degenerated into a knockabout on stage. This was not a harp showcase number.

No.5, a cheerful light number, had potential but her own part was just blocky chords, like a cut-down piano part.

Ah, no.6. This was it. Schubert's first duet with The Girl. After a few lines of undistinguished introduction, a soaring romantic slow waltz duet. There was not all that much in her part except a few rising-quaver motifs. But music was what you made it; she shaped the phrases by careful choice of how, and where on the string, she plucked each note. She held the quavers back, delaying the completion of the chords, shaping the dynamics, reining the singers in, raising the emotional temperature, until the mood of the duet could be felt even in the back row of the gallery. The thin Wednesday audience came alive, clapping and cheering.

Soon it was the main interval, and she declined the MD's invitation to tea for all in the bandroom, in favour of retuning. During this task, she reflected on how sociable a pit was, yet unsociable at the same time. All these hours near her friend the bass, but she'd have to twist round and he to lean forwards if they were to chat. The cellist was next to her but with the harp itself between them. Her music stand hid the viola player directly in front of her except for his collar, and all she could see of the violinists in front of her was the backs of their heads. The wind players opposite were quite hidden except for occasional glimpses of the clarinettist's nose and the oboist's ear. The strings were quite a pleasant bunch once you got through their permanently gloomy introspection, and the woodwind were positive fun when not scraping their reeds or holding them anxiously up to the light. The brass and percussion were lively but a bit gung-ho for this slushy sentimental show. How was it that only harpists were normal and cheerful? Was it to do with the glorious radiant sound that harps made, fit for the gods, superior to any other orchestral instrument?

The second Act went adequately. There was nothing special for the harp until the Second Act Finale, in which the plot, drama and music all suddenly picked up. It was one of the best pre-interval finales she had ever known.

The second interval was too short for her to retune, and therefore it didn't matter greatly that she couldn't identify any harp lollipops in the following short third Act; that Act seemed mainly there to patch up the character of the man who steals the heroine from Schubert and to confirm Schubert as a thoroughly Good Chap, who continues to make sacrifices to ensure the happiness of the girl he has just lost. *Lilac Time* was unusual in that the hero does *not* get the girl.

Thursday went as well as her preparations deserved, but she

still vaguely felt something was missing. She could not put her finger on it.

At the end of the performance, she had to remove her harp, and all her bits and pieces, from the pit to go to Friday's funeral. The dep should find everything in order, with the harp part marked up in soft pencil with all the pedal changes, some of which were not what you would expect at all from just looking at the key changes.

Arriving in the pit breathless from having misjudged the journey time, the gawky-looking girl who was the dep pulled off her harp's coat. Then she threw off her own, to reveal her glamorous black concert dress. She then let down her hair, which framed her gently flushed face. The trombonist and trumpeter gasped at the transformation into beautiful young woman, and exchanged graphic descriptions of the fantasies which she had unknowingly evoked.

Also the MD sat open-mouthed in admiration. She was so similar to the regular player, except even more beautiful. Medium height, as slim as a sylph, perfect figure and complexion, striking long blonde hair, elegant well-shaped arms and hands, the very picture of delicate beauty, yet doubtless as strong as an ox to cart her harp about. Why was it, he wondered, that all harpists looked exactly the same? And how come they all seemed to be about 22 years old? What happened to them all when they reached 30? Where did they all vanish to?

Out of tune, the dep played the first Act with restraint, to the especial surprise of the singers in no.6, who were expecting their song to be shaped for them by the harp. By the interval, the dep was almost dizzy from the task of sight-reading her part in live performance, and turned with relief to the task of tuning.

Her brain now in gear, the dep played the second Act with a steady noble authority and an even consistent plucking technique. Nobody said anything to her, but she began to get an inkling that this was not how the regular harp had played, from the occasional hesitations by the singers on-stage. Therefore, for the Second Act Finale, she abandoned her neutral impersonal style and let her feelings mould her playing. Warned by a pencilled note in her part that the interval was only a few minutes, she stayed seated in the pit.

"Say," shouted a young bearded man over the pit rail, "that was good. I don't go for this music, I nearly went home after the First Act, but here, in this Act, you gave it something all right."

She went up to her side of the rail and said, "Thanks, but who are you, musician or what?"

"But you remember me?" exclaimed the man. "You hitched a lift from me at the petrol station."

"What *are* you talking about?"

"You mean.., no, it's really not you at all, oh dear, I'm sorry, let me explain." The interval bell rang. "I'll come up at the end and tell you the whole story. Over a drink maybe."

"Yes, why not, I'm all frazzled from having got here. I could do with a break before I set off home."

At the end, he came up and watched her pack her harp.

"I'll carry your things," he offered, "but I won't help you with your harp, I think you probably know what you're doing better than me."

What a considerate and knowledgeable man, she thought.

On the Saturday afternoon, the regular harpist returned and re-established herself on the harp seat. Tired from her long overnight journey from the funeral, she played the matinée on autopilot. The singers, too, were performing with restraint, husbanding their voices for the evening.

In the break between the houses, she took a nap in the pit, curled up on her padded harp coat. As word spread, many of the theatre staff tiptoed up, one by one, to admire this sight.

She woke with a new determination to solve the problem of dull intonation during her big numbers. By that stage of the show, the heat and humidity had sent her pitch flat while the wind had gone sharp. All quite usual but, tonight, she would no longer accept it as inevitable. She would compensate by tuning sharp. This was supposed to be terribly bad for the soundboard, but it was a newish harp, it should take it. A fraction of a semitone should be enough. Now to guess exactly how sharp to go, to match the pitch of the wind at no.6 …

Disoriented by her brighter sound, and by the fact that her Fs were inexplicably not as sharp as all her other notes, she missed her entrance to no.2. This was a trio by the heroine and her two sisters. The trio seemed to start after a different cue each night, and the harpist began to suspect the girls were ad-libbing. Whatever the reason, it was a pity, as other MDs were very possibly in the audience, and she so wanted to make a good impression.

Although she had overcompensated and was still slightly sharp even by no.6, she gave it all she had. The singers were no longer with her, seemingly having forgotten Wednesday's triumph. This was getting worrying, if she was to put the harp on every MD's must-have list. And an annoying buzz had set in. At the interval, she was grateful to get out of the pit and have a congenial chat, her last of the week, in the bandroom.

The Second Act Finale would be the place to make her mark. It had something for everybody, on stage and in the pit.

A few seconds before this Finale was reached, her G-above-middle-C string broke near the top. She just had time to push the string downwards and grope for it through the access hole concealed behind the soundboard. Luckily, she felt it at once and pulled out the broken end.

She anxiously shot her eyes along her part, where she had to cope with five different keys before even the first page turn. She worked out that she could cover the G♯ in her third chord by an A♭ if she remembered to correct the A♭ for A♮ in time for the very next chord. There were a few unavoidable Gs which she would have to omit in the following triplet passage, but this, she remembered, more or less duplicated the string parts, so she would not be missed. The G-flats would have to be covered by F-sharps, as long as she could lift her F pedal back up to F♮ by the very next beat.

And so it went on, a constant battle of mental arithmetic and juggling of which notes were essential, which she could substitute by others an octave away, and which could be safely omitted. She even had to break the rules and use her little finger to improvise some of the chords. She was too busy to notice that her relatively flat F, when pedalled to F♯, was now making a perfectly tempered G♭. She did however notice that the buzz had cured itself; it must have been the G string on the point of breaking.

As the end came in sight, she had a thirty-bar breather while the cello milked his big solo, another theme from the Unfinished Symphony. It covers the poignant moments when Schubert on stage has to absorb the fact that his own song, sung by his own best friend, has taken his girl friend away from him.

Normally the harpist resented the cellist's over-emotion, but tonight she welcomed it taking the heat off her. It gave her time to unwind the top end of the broken string before it tangled and caused trouble. All this was on that side of the harp away from the audience and lit by stray light from the stage, lucky she had refused to move at the beginning of the week.

Then just a few chords, and a glissando – the second in the same scene – to signal the end-of-act curtain. Even the glissando had to be carefully phrased, with a diminuendo to conceal that the G was missing, before a decisive final flourish.

The second interval, though only five minutes, would give her time to replace her G string. First, a quick dash to the backstage Ladies – but she still had to queue – then back to the pit. Look out the relevant spare string, the felt pad rescued from the broken string, a gut tag, her trimming scissors and her tuning key.

She was in the course of tying the end of the new string into that special harpists' securing knot that is nowhere listed in the Boy Scout's Book of Knots, when two faces appeared over the pit rail.

"Hello, wish us happiness, you brought us together," said the bearded young man, lovingly clasping the dep.

"Yes, isn't it all a wonderful coincidence!" added the dep. "And your playing – it added so much – you've given me something to aim for now. It was like you were playing for us!"

"Have a drink with us afterwards," said the man; the dep giggled.

"Yes, I hope you'll be very happy, I'm pleased for you," she said faintly. She knew now what Father Zell felt like on-stage when his daughters rushed off finding men, with him being the last to know. She was too weak with surprise to fit the new string by the time the house lights dimmed. Concentrate on the music, girl.

No.18 in the generally lacklustre third Act suddenly had a new resonance for her. After a few bars' rest while other musicians played under dialogue, she had fine pealing upwards arpeggios which were supposed to begin, and tonight they did exactly, when the heroine starts to wonder aloud whether her dubious new man really has turned over a new leaf. Then more wonderful arpeggios – she'd never appreciated them before – as Schubert and the heroine (his ex-girl) reprise the title song that Schubert had written for her.

The gods must be on her side, as the piece was in the key of five flats and the missing G occurred as a natural in only one place, all other occurrences being able to be covered by F-sharps. And the F-sharps were in tune for G♭. More than that, her initial sharpness was now exactly matching the pitch that the wind had reached.

All the dramatic devices couldn't disguise what a fraught match the heroine had made for herself. While the harpist wondered whether her dep's romance was equally shaky or would last, her concentration lapsed and she messed up a couple of the many awkward and quick-fire pedal changes required by the harmonic modulations of the song.

In the Finale Ultimo and curtain calls, she couldn't be heard through the orchestra. So her last audible contribution had ruined the entire impression she had spent all week trying to build up. Her normally sunny temperament disintegrated as she wondered whether they'd ever book a harp again after this mess-up, knowing that even if they did, it wouldn't be her.

She listened to the end-of-run speeches on stage in an untypical miserable daze, wanting only to curl up and be forgotten. The MD conducted the playout from the stage, where he had taken his bow. As she played again, her mood started to bounce back, so much so that on the last note, she exuberantly played not one but three glissandi, plus a few extra chords. A few people stopped putting on their coats to applaud.

The MD returned to the pit to thank everybody, as the musicians started slowly to pack up. There was often a reluctance to hurry away if the week had gone well.

The MD worked his way along the pit to the harpist, and, to her, he said, "Your dep was good ..."

At which, her self-confidence plunged back to rock-bottom.

She hardly heard the MD continue, "... but she didn't *feel* the music like you do. It matters, you see. Because this company's just won a lottery grant to put on a Puccini cycle starting in the autumn. Can I put your name down as harp for all of them?"

The Clarinettists

"Who's for a picnic by the river?" shouted the second violinist the instant the MD lowered his baton.

The meagre Saturday matinée audience had long since filed out of the auditorium, but the orchestra dutifully played to the end of the playout. It had been stiflingly hot this last day or two, exceptionally hot, unbelievable for springtime.

Only the two clarinettists agreed to join the picnic, because, in this small Scottish county town, most of the orchestra lived close enough to go home before the evening performance, the last of this run of *Princess Ida*.

Led by the violinist, the three reached a spot on the riverbank sometimes frequented by salmon fishermen but deserted today. After they had shared out their packed teas, the violinist said she wanted to take a cooling dip in the river.

"For goodness sake no!" shouted the first clarinettist. "Look how fast it's flowing. And there's nowhere for you to change."

"Nonsense, I'll swim in my underwear. It's so warm that I'll be dry in no time when I come out. And don't snigger, I'm old enough to be your mother."

With those words, she stripped off her black outerwear and plunged in. To the clarinettist's consternation, she seemed to make no effort to swim but let the current carry her downstream.

He immediately jumped in after her. Ouch, he had never imagined that the water would be so bitterly numbingly cold. It was all he could do to stay conscious, but somehow he rallied himself to swim to her and push her to the bank.

"Don't blame yourself, you did all the right things," said the ambulanceman afterwards. "This weather has thawed the snow fields on the hills, but everyone forgets the meltwater's still ice-cold. It looks like the cold shock gave her a fatal heart attack. Young fit chap drowned here yesterday, you know. Anyway, here's the police to interview you, all the usual stuff."

"Usual stuff, indeed," said the one clarinettist to the other. "It may be 'usual' if you're an ambulanceman, but what happens now? We don't even know exactly who she was."

"Well, let's go back and open her violin case. We might find something there to identify her."

The police escorted the clarinettists back to the theatre. The auditorium was unexpectedly chilly, as the theatre management had hired in portable air-conditioners to prepare for the evening house. As the first clarinettist could not continue in his wet clothes in this cold, the wardrobe mistress conjured up a change of dry black clothes for him. He wondered how his wife would take all this, as she was easily unsettled by anything out of the ordinary.

Under the watchful eye of the police, the clarinettists then opened the dead violinist's case. Instead of a simple name-and-address label as they had hoped, there, clipped to the inside of the lid, was a whole gallery of group photographs and concert programmes, relics of her past triumphs.

The first item to catch their eye was a faded photograph of a string quartet; that glamorous violinist in it was just recognisable, across the decades, as her. Next to this was a yellowing concert review, cut out from a newspaper long ago. And there was an old programme, brittle with age, for a concert featuring Mozart's Sinfonia Concertante for violin and viola. Out of the programme fell the fragile remains of a dried rose.

The first clarinettist was meanwhile engrossed by that quartet photograph, on which the viola player looked very like an old college picture of his own father. No wonder: the old programme, when carefully opened out, showed his father's name as viola soloist. His father had occasionally hinted at a great lost love. The rose …?

The clarinettists confirmed to the police that they lived in the same city, an hour away from this town, that they were sharing lifts this week, that they were college contemporaries who, though not particularly friends, often found themselves thrown together professionally like this.

The MD, arriving early for the Saturday evening house, broke in upon this scene. Surprised to see a policeman in the pit, he confirmed the violinist's name – the same as on that old programme. He was stunned to learn what had happened to her, but collected himself enough to demand no further police questioning now until the end of the show. In return, the police insisted on leaving a constable to stay with the orchestra. If only, thought the MD, he could always have a policeman in the pit to stop the brass players disappearing to the pub!

One by one, unsuspecting and all shocked as they individually were told, the rest of the orchestra arrived in the pit. Subdued by the police presence, and upset by the careless chatter of the cheerful audience, the orchestra – depleted by this sudden death – was in no mood to play. But they knew they had to carry on as if nothing had happened.

The leader asked to see inside the dead violinist's case, and reverentially lifted the velvet cloth to reveal the silent violin. He gently touched it with his fingertips. Before replacing the cloth and closing the case, he seemed to be muttering words of condolence to it. The second clarinettist laughed aloud at this affectation.

To make the second violinist's empty desk less prominent, somebody unplugged her music stand light, but this only served to accentuate her absence. Eventually, the MD decided to carry her chair and music stand out of the pit, and asked everybody to shuffle up to fill the gap. The ever-watchful policeman confiscated the band part off the stand in case it contained anything personal of hers.

The second clarinettist noticed how, without the second-violin desk, the pit looked different, in that he could now see all the way through to the cellist. He'd never really noticed him before, certainly would never have recognised him. As he looked more around him, he noticed a number of other unfamiliar faces too, deps perhaps.

The orchestra tuned up but with none of the usual warm-up runs and trills. Out of habit, very necessary with their chilly clarinets this evening, both clarinettists breathed down their instruments to ensure an even temperature, and hence reliable intonation, later. They concentrated more on their B♭ clarinets, these being used for all of the first seven or eight numbers.

As the house lights dimmed, the MD entered. As the spotlight caught him, he forced a smile onto his lips and bowed to the audience.

Turning then to the orchestra, he whispered, "Dreadful for you all, I know, but I expect she'd have wanted us to carry on tonight. OK, go for it."

This would be the eighth time this week that the first clarinettist had played this music through, but in his state of shock it was as if he had never seen it before. The lively opening of the overture swept him along.

Then a few bars' rest before his first solo of the evening, a foretaste of Princess Ida's first big song. Breathe in. No, the mouthpiece felt wrong as he reclosed his lips over it. He whipped the clarinet out of his mouth to check that it really was his. Big mistake. He had about half a second left to re-establish his embouchure before his opening mid-stave A. Fearing he would get a squeak an octave-and-a-half above the A, he tightened his lips and was dumbfounded to hear the G *below*.

His eye dashed ahead, and, leaning back to give himself space, he waggled his clarinet bell pointing at a quaver's rest at the end of this phrase, hoping desperately that his colleague would take the hint and play the 'first's' line from that point, just safely ahead of the next dangerous A.

This is where he regretted his persistently holier-than-thou attitude. His colleague the second clarinettist was always ready for a game, suggesting playing alternate notes each, playing on the wrong clarinet, swapping lines between the two of them, anything for a laugh. The first clarinettist had always dourly scotched such ideas. And now he would pay for it.

But he couldn't work out what was going wrong. Yes, he had forgotten the notes to the extent that it felt like sight-reading, but he hadn't forgotten elementary fingering, hardly, not yet. He *knew* he had done everything right for that A. So pre-occupied that he missed the second clarinettist fluently taking over at the indicated spot, he inspected the operation of the A key. All in order. The second clarinettist (playing first) was now frantically elbowing his colleague, as an important counter-melody, including the suspect A, lay ahead.

In the nick of time, the first clarinettist's brain clicked into gear: in this chill, his breath was condensing on the inside of his clarinet and forming a film of water. This must be blocking the holes controlled by the A key. Nothing for it, in this extremity, but to hold his clarinet sideways and blow through the A key hole mouthorgan-style. Gently, or the noise would be too distracting.

When that same note next occurred in the countermelody, he played it tentatively, just as well; he had only partly cleared the problem and was rewarded with a G♯, just half as wrong as before. Here he was, three minutes into the show, and he'd already had enough excitement, mistakes and worry to last a week, not even counting the fateful picnic. And there was his colleague, exquisitely phrasing a solo trill as if his whole life had been spent preparing for it.

He had a few moments to dab at the suspect holes with cigarette papers slid under the keys to blot away the offending internal condensation before no.3, when he would have a short solo, on the same clarinet.

Should he chicken out and revert to playing the 'second' line? Or should he, for safety, try it on his A clarinet? Transposing at sight was just the sort of game his second clarinettist would enjoy. Even tonight. How could someone be so unruffled? he wondered, looking sidelong at him. His lifestyle was so different. Gilbert & Sullivan was as serious as he ever got, he was most at home out with the lads on a pub crawl or playing alto saxophone in some smoky club. Had this hardened him against the shocks of today?

No further time for these reflections now, the MD was already conducting no.3 and, with no time left to change clarinets, he would have to use the (correct) B♭ clarinet. The solo was in tune, perfect. Phew.

The next few numbers went well, and by this time the first clarinettist's memory of the music was returning, so that he was prepared for the tricky offbeat contrapuntal triplets in no.5.

A few minutes later, they had already reached the First Act Finale. He remembered how he had caused the band call to collapse at this very number, through no fault of his. After a recitative, his part had a solo quaver passage completely absent from the piano reduction which had been used by their rehearsal accompanist. These unexpected notes had confused the singers into silence.

But the singers were on form for the First Act Finale tonight. When, after self-consciously correct playing by the band, the curtain fell, the musicians all quickly filed out of the pit. The policeman made to prevent this mass escape of potential inquest witnesses, but the MD reassured him that nobody, not even the clarinettists, would vanish, least of all between Acts; on the contrary, they would not only diligently finish the show, they would remain traceable afterwards, because their livelihoods depended on it.

The bar turned out to be the warmest place in the over-chilled theatre, and the bandsmen luxuriated in it, almost able to forget about their drowned colleague.

Unwillingly they obeyed the summons of the interval bell, and tuned up for the second Act. This did not start well. On-stage, a door jammed and the top came off a chair. The actors, distracted, confused some of their lines and omitted to say the cues that the musicians had come to rely on as warnings to pick up their instruments and prepare to play. One of the deps played in prominently the wrong key, while another was lost and his silence made the sound offputtingly different.

All these minor errors were infectious throughout the band. The first clarinettist missed an instruction in his part to change to the A clarinet for no.12. Suspecting some mechanical failure in his clarinet, he wasted valuable time before realising his mistake and switching his brain to transpose his part down a semitone at sight.

This brought back memories of his boyhood when his family could afford to buy him only one clarinet, and for years he had to play A-clarinet parts on his B♭ instrument, as he was again doing now. Here was something string players never had to contend with, changing an instrument mid-song. They didn't even have to control their breathing, why, a breath in the wrong place could upset your embouchure and ruin the intonation of the following notes. Yet string players did nothing but complain about strings, bows, you name it, when on *their* instruments they could pitch any note exactly how they liked. And when they weren't complaining, they would be talking in this super-polite precious superior way to each other. Come to think of it, that's what set that second violinist apart, she was quite normal and friendly and not at all snooty. She really would be missed.

Soon, the MD was lifting his baton for no.14, which starts with a lovely slow clarinet solo foreshadowing Ida's line, which she sings with the three men, disguised as women, who have joined her university.

Taking care that he had attached his mouthpiece to the A clarinet this time, the first clarinettist played his solo with lyrical and melting beauty, until a high E on the very last semiquaver of the second bar sounded odd. Never mind, plough on, he was sure he'd fingered it right. Four times did that high E recur in the very next bar, and every time it sounded like D♯. Luckily the offending note did not then recur for some time.

It would be so simple if he could bring himself to believe that the drowned violinist had cast some spell, but he was a rational man and realised there must be a more practical explanation. On a hunch, he silently trilled his A♭/E♭ key, and yes, the key felt soggy, which confirmed his suspicion that its tiny spring, which spent year after year quietly pressing its key to shut the hole, had finally given up the ghost.

Well, that was easy. His fellow clarinettists, especially this week's second clarinettist, were always ridiculing his extensive tool kit. Let them laugh, he had in stock several elastic bands, replaced by rota before they went brittle, one of which was exactly the size for winding from the bottom key post, up across the offending key, and round the thumb rest. Probably there would be no more high E notes in the part, but never mind, his systematic and orderly maintenance routines were paying dividends.

His self-righteous glow began to fade during the next dialogue, as it was clear that the unsteadiness within the band had communicated itself to the actors. He found his experience as a player was unravelling – he was now having to work out the fingering of each note as he read it. Fortunately, both clarinets in no.14 were in unison, and even more fortunately, his second clarinettist (unlike himself) was playing better than ever.

He whispered to his colleague, "Sorry, I can't cope with all this, will you play 'first'?"

"Sure, no trouble."

Even playing the 'second' line, all was not well. Time and again he was hitting wrong notes, not squeaks a twelfth sharp, which would be explained if his lips were not engaging the mouthpiece properly, but notes just a semitone or two sharp.

During the next dialogue, he silently practised the fingering of the following number, and felt something slack. Incredible. As if his other misfortunes weren't enough, now the ring assembly on his bottom joint had failed. He was happy that his own fingering was not to blame for his last batch of wrong notes but incredulous to be suffering a third mechanical failure inside an hour.

He looked for the tiny grub screw at each end of his ring assembly, and the lower one was ... gone. No hope of finding it on this cluttered dimly lit floor. A violin would always limp on, it was glued, not held together by inadequate screws that got lost, it surely would never let you down like this.

Sighing, he pulled out his A clarinet and decided to play the rest of the show on that. Transpose everything *up* a semitone this time. At least, the mental effort would take his mind off things. Ah, good, they had reached no.20 already, the Second Act Finale, which meant an interval soon, to grab a drink and relax a bit, and then just a short third Act.

The MD gave the beat to start no.20. Silence, followed by some ragged entries, before the whole number collapsed in an ignominious heap. The MD cursed himself for overlooking that no.20 begins with semiquavers played solo on the second violin, the very instrument that was so tragically missing.

"Start from bar 5," hissed the MD desperately, "a bar for

nothing ..," and shakily the show continued.

In the second interval, though the orchestra had been asked to remain seated in the pit, the second clarinettist was in such desperate need of a drink that he dashed out to the bar before the policeman could stop him. Meanwhile, with it being so cold, the first clarinettist couldn't wait through another whole Act before using the Gents, so he too dashed out.

Backstage, he came upon Princess Ida combing out her long auburn stage wig. He was struck by her real hair, and wondered whether he dare tell her it was more attractive than her wig, when she turned and noticed him. Recognising him as a musician, she scowled at him, an unexpected change from her radiant on-stage smile.

"What's going on down there?" she demanded. "You're worse than a school orchestra!"

"Oh," he replied, "we're missing the second violinist," and without thinking he added, "She just drowned during a picnic by the river."

"Ah," replied Princess Ida, "so I *did* see a policeman in the pit. The violinist, who was she?"

Princess Ida was shocked by the answer. That violinist had been a most effective behind-the-scenes lobbyist for women's opportunities in music education. Few people knew that she had founded the very voice training scholarship that had propelled Ida into soloistic league. Her death was a sore loss.

In Ida's last big song, a few minutes into that final Act, bewailing the collapse of all her dreams for women's education, Ida poured everything into it. The lighting crew sensed that there was something special going on, and dimmed the lights sensitively, which had not been in the lighting plot for the week.

The word spread backstage, and the remaining (mostly humorous) numbers were played with a subdued dignity, which the audience could not understand. They responded well, however, to the convincingly sung and played Finale, whose theme is that a happy resolution is possible even amidst shattered hopes. A few bars into this, the second clarinettist, playing first, had a short solo, which he played well to all outward appearances.

But he whispered to his principal, "I can't do this solo again in the curtain call. You take over again please. It's on the A clarinet anyway."

And so it was, the two clarinettists back to their rightful places, breathing and phrasing together, impeccable intonation, but not much cheer in the pit nor applause from the audience.

This operatic company did not indulge in last-night speeches from the stage, nor, as independent-minded Scots, did they hold with playing the National Anthem, so it was straight into the Playout, being the music (sometimes alternatively known as the Exit Music or Chaser or Outmarch) which is played as the house lights rise and which is meant to send the audience on their way whistling the tunes. In this production, the playout was the Overture.

While it is traditional not to use the playout provided in the hired music but for the MD to cobble one together from numbers of his own choosing, the Overture was a most unusual choice, especially as Sullivan never wrote playouts and G&S is therefore hardly ever played with playouts anyway.

After a good loud opening, the overture/playout quotes quiet songs in minor keys, including Ida's first big song, a sad and contemplative number invoking the goddess of wisdom. This matched the orchestra's mood exactly, and they played with an intensity which carried to the audience. They stopped shuffling their coats and car-keys, stood still and listened intently to the end.

The policeman had by now come to accept that the musicians would really not abscond. When his radio crackled with a request for assistance at a pub brawl, he was quite glad of the excuse to allow everyone to go home.

The first clarinettist immediately sought out the wardrobe mistress backstage to reclaim his wet clothes. To his pleasant surprise, she had managed to dry them out and, at the risk of his second clarinettist's grumbles at the delay, he changed back into them there and then, checking for his car keys.

He was relieved that he would not now have to explain wet clothes, or a set of borrowed clothing, to his wife. And with any luck, she would already be fast asleep by the time he got in.

He was astonished to find his second clarinettist, far from impatiently itching to be driven to his drinking binge, quietly using the wait to clean and polish the mechanism of his clarinets, something he had never before been seen to do.

The first clarinettist dropped his colleague outside his favourite night club and drove on home.

As he slipped quietly into bed beside his wife, she half woke and asked dreamily, "Oh, you're back, that's nice, how did it go? Anything happen?"

"Oh, it was all fine," he replied, "nothing unusual at all. Sleep tight."

Meanwhile the second clarinettist at his night club had bumped into an old drinking partner, who greeted him with delight: "You've just finished a show tonight? C'mon then, let's get totally pissed, then we'll get seriously drunk. Then we'll celebrate. What'll you have to start with?"

"Oh, well, I don't know, somehow I'm not in the mood after all, I'm off home to bed."

The Second Violinist

In a rare quiet moment, her mind turned to the evening, far away from this soul-destroying telephone call centre. She would be playing her violin for *La Traviata* in the pit of the theatre in …

Her light came on. "Thank-you-for-phoning-Domestic-Insurance-my-name-is-Jane[it wasn't]-how-may-I-help," she intoned mechanically for the twentieth time that day. It felt like the hundredth. "House-insurance-yes-what-is-your-postcode-please." Extraordinary, it was the same as her married address had been. "Is-that-Hill-Crescent-what-is-your-house-number."

Oh, horror, it was her ex-husband.

She had first met him in a pit. He was sitting next to her, playing the viola. They were immediately attracted to each other and married soon afterwards. She was so in love that it was all the more of a shock to her when he started to flaunt mistresses in front of her. In this and other ways, he belittled her in public until she had lost any sense of self-worth. The divorce had been so acrimonious that …

An automatic reminder flashed on her screen, prompting her through the questions. What lies he was telling about the property! Without changing her voice, she slipped in a question of her own: "What-are-the-names-of-the-persons-apart-from-yourself-who-are-residing-at-the-property?"

Well! How could he! Of all the loose-living floosies, he had to shack up with *that* one! Illogical perhaps, but she felt degraded and polluted.

Her supervisor had been listening in and sent her home at once in disgrace. She didn't mind, apart from the few hours' money she had lost, because it gave her plenty of time to change, eat and travel to the theatre, instead of the usual mad rush.

The theatre was warm and welcoming. There was a stage door that she was supposed to use, but it was a long way round with awkward steps. She always preferred the atmosphere and sense of anticipation of the public foyer, from which an unobtrusive door led directly backstage.

She loved this theatre. She had haunted it since her music student days and had done some of her earliest gigs here. Nothing had ever been changed. It was a secure beacon in her life. On one wall backstage, just inside that door from the foyer, there was a pattern of cracks in the plaster in almost exactly the shape of a saxophone, and, it must have been decades ago, someone had pencilled on the wall a sketch of a man, in the posture of playing this imaginary saxophone. It had never been painted over or replastered. Seeing it always made her smile.

She climbed down a few steps from a corridor into the pit. This was her world. Dark and warm, the pit gave her a womb-like security and reassurance. Each player sat in his own private pool of light cast by his music stand, independent, respected by the others as a master, yet all co-operating far closer than any team sportsman could imagine.

Here she was safe from the irritations of the world. No phone would ring, no supervisor would scold her, no postman would deliver bills to her here ... The work down here might be difficult, even at the limit of her abilities, but it was self-contained, defined by the notes in front of her. She could not be asked to squeeze any other tasks in, or to speed up her rate of work.

And above all, in the pit, she was Somebody. In the

outside world, she was nobody. Since her mother died, she was nobody's daughter. She was not anybody's mother and now she was no longer even anybody's wife. Unless she was in a pit, or had a future pit engagement in her diary, she felt unwanted and useless.

In the rural county where she grew up, her mother had been a violin teacher and played regularly for two of the four amateur operatic companies based in the county. The orchestras hardly ever changed, except as required by the instrumentation of the particular show. Everybody active in those circles knew everybody else. Once you were in, and that could mean waiting years for someone already in to retire or die, you yourself were safely there for life.

What a difference the daughter found when she graduated from her London music college! She soon realised she had no hope of landing a permanent job as a violinist; such jobs hardly ever came up any more. Even occasional gigs were a rarity.

So here she was, stuck in a menial job in a market town that had become absorbed into the outer London commuter belt. Although there were easily twenty amateur operatic companies within reasonable travelling distance, and hence plenty of pit work around, she was in fierce competition for it with other jobless London-college music graduates, with players on the fringes of the great London orchestras and with the many superbly proficient semi-professional players that a world metropolis attracts. She was so rarely asked to play in a pit that she savoured her rare weeks there all the more.

The odds had, however, been more in her favour to be offered this week of *La Traviata*, because instead of the three or so violins typical in a show, the orchestration of *La Traviata* requires no fewer than eight of them. She was pleasantly surprised to find this number of violins when she arrived at the band call on the Sunday morning, and even more pleased to find she knew some of them already, though not the leader.

"Hello everybody," the MD welcomed them. "Thanks, all of you, for turning up so punctually at this ungodly time. I expect you're wondering about the unusual rehearsal timetable, two band calls today and then two dress rehearsals. It's not that I've any doubts about you. Or about the singers. What it is, you see, is that Violetta's role is far more strenuous than anything in your average Gilbert & Sullivan or Rodgers & Hammerstein, and you couldn't expect an amateur singer to sing it all through, each night of the week. So they've cast two Violettas, singing just some nights each. And of course each Violetta has to have a bandcall and a dress rehearsal. Hard work for you I know, but remember, all profits from this show are going to an AIDS charity. OK, you've tuned up, let's get on, overture please."

The first notes of a bandcall are usually rough and dreadful, as the players have not warmed up yet and may be sight-reading unfamiliar music. Those not familiar with the MD's beat may even fail to begin at all, or may misread his beat and play at exactly twice or half the intended tempo.

The second violinist was expecting all this when, on the downbeat, the Preludio started with perfect ensemble and intonation, played with hushed atmospheric beauty, by just the violins, divided into eight lines, playing muted. It was ravishing. The viola player was so astounded and moved that he failed to enter after his seven bars' rest. On the next attempt, the opening went perfectly. She had never known a week's show to start as promisingly as this. All the various mistakes and problems that cropped up throughout that long day of two complete runs-through were laughed off as minor in context. The violins were the stars of this band and she was one of them.

Returning to the present, the week so far had had its ups and downs, but she continued to be pleased. Here she was in the pit, free from her day-job worries for a few more hours, making great music. She even forgave the telephone call centre for having sent her home early that day.

The principal singers had got it together as well as could ever be imagined, and the band, over half of whom were strings and most of them violins, were playing as responsively and gently as a fine permanent professional chamber orchestra. Her own performance was about as neat and faultless as she had ever played anything. Even Giorgio had been convincing, in the difficult task of warning Violetta off his son for reasons which a 21st-century audience would normally dismiss as absurd. If the plot were updated to have Violetta suffering from AIDS, it would become more believable. Ah, is that why this was all for an AIDS charity?

Anyway, if the AIDS charity could be paid by the quality of the music, she thought, they should do very well out of this week. This, the Thursday performance, had really been quite brilliant. Having exchanged "Goodnight, see you tomorrow, yes wasn't it good" with her fellow players, she sailed homewards in her car. It seemed to drive itself, at effortless high speed. After two near misses in traffic and wafting happily straight through a red light, she realised she was in such a state of euphoria she was a public hazard.

She woke up the next morning, Friday, with a dreadful headache. She felt weary. The patch of hard skin on the left underside of her chin, where so many violinists have a bruise or callus from their chinrests, was tender and chafed. Resigned, she dabbed on lotion and, struggling against her weariness, made herself remove the chinrest from her violin and wipe it with disinfectant. While she was at it, before setting off for her call centre, she took her shoulder rest out of her violin case to remind herself to replace its protective rubber sleeves, which were cracked and nearly worn through.

She was so drowsy that her brain felt as if it was

disconnected. Paradoxically, this helped her get through the day's work. She didn't think, she just mindlessly let the computer screen in front of her guide her step by step. Her supervisor even broke in between calls to compliment her on her efficiency and correctness, some kind of apology for yesterday she supposed. Somehow she got herself to the theatre that evening and, as she walked into the foyer, through the private door to backstage and past the man-and-saxophone, she began to feel her fatigue slipping away.

The viola player greeted her cheerfully, "Gosh, you look dreadful, have a chocolate!"

She felt better for it. He had in fact been showing her small kindnesses all week. Also, she had enjoyed listening to his viola playing, she had never heard anyone as good. She was just thinking how she would miss him after the end of the week, when he mentioned that this was already his last night; he was having to send a dep tomorrow.

As they went into the pit and she took her violin out of her case to tune up, she saw – no chinrest, no shoulder rest. Both still at home. This was a major crisis. Without a chinrest, you were merely uncomfortable but could still play. Without a shoulder rest, you'd lost all your accustomed stability in holding the violin, and you risked dropping it into your lap if you tried a fast shift down to first position. Fine if you stayed in first, but it needed just a moment's forgetfulness ...

What a stupid instrument the violin was. It was a life sentence to learn it, and she'd only chosen it because of her mother's example. It was totally non-ergonomic: pianos had keys spaced for a player's convenience, a clarinet had its holes controlled by keys connected through long levers to group them together for a player's convenience, a drum had sticks with handles designed for a player's convenience, a trumpet had its pipework organised so that the valves were next to each other and easy to manipulate, only the wretched violin was designed with total disregard for ease of playing, demanding painful and strained postures. Even the bow was awkward to use properly.

You could never play this cruel and confounded instrument well. As you progressed, you would learn to play less and less out of tune, and you would split fewer and fewer of the notes, but you could never do better than avoid mistakes. And when you became the best violinist in your school, you found you were still only good in the county youth orchestra, average at music college, and finally unemployable at professional level. Her headache was threatening to return. Without her shoulder rest, what was she to do?

The viola player, having taken in her predicament at a glance, re-appeared in a minute or two with a long narrow towel which he had swept off the theatre bar-top before anyone could stop him.

"It might smell a bit of beer, but if you fold it like this round your violin and use this elastic band ...," and in a moment had improvised a shoulder rest for her.

In relief, she tuned up and tried a few shifts, upwards *then downwards*. Yes, it would do. And in a moment, the lights went down and the MD tapped for silence to begin the Preludio.

The eight-violins-divisi opening seemed to sing straight to heaven. The rest of the performance continued on this impossibly high level, the other Violetta bringing a different but equally valid interpretation to the piece. It was rare enough for a violinist outside the professional opera houses to have the chance to play *La Traviata* and surely unique to participate in such a memorable performance.

Driving home, she recognised the viola player's car in front of her, and she managed to draw alongside him in a traffic queue, hoping he would look sideways and notice her.

He did. They waved enthusiastically to each other before the parallel traffic lanes moved off at different speeds, separating them.

Knowing from experience how heavy Saturday traffic could be, she set off early for the matinée. But she had never known it this bad. The traffic seized up solid about a mile from the theatre, and with still over half an hour to spare, she wondered about parking her car just anywhere and walking. The traffic then eased a little and, as she inched past some railings, she looked through and saw that her favourite secret parking space on a piece of waste ground was already occupied. She would have pay the extortionate parking charges of the town centre. But there, even the short-term multi-storey car park had a queue. She arrived at the theatre, just on the dot. But they weren't ready to start.

About five minutes later, the percussionist rushed in, all apologies, panting and sweating.

"OK," the MD whispered to the orchestra, "all present now except the viola, and who'll notice? It's only a dep anyway. Let's start, then we'll still have a decent rest before the evening house."

The leader gestured to the cellist to move forwards to occupy the viola seat, so that the viola, when he did arrive, could sit down unobtrusively at the back in the cello seat, without a disruptive trek into the centre of the pit during the performance. The second violinist, used to having the viola join her in the off-the-beat accompaniment figures, was at first confused by the unaccustomed cello line of music being played next to her, including some solos and duets with the leader.

However the cellist, used to sitting at the back of the string section, said this unusual seat was as good as sitting in the principal's seat in a symphony orchestra: he was so close he could effortlessly read the MD's beat without peering into distant gloom and having to pray that none of the players in front of him had fidgeted or shuffled into his narrow line of sight. Better still for him, here he was surrounded in every direction by musicians creating the other strands of the music all around him.

When the lights rose for the first interval, the leader stood up, looked round and announced, "Well, just fancy, we do have a viola now, not that I heard him at all. Wonder when he arrived. You'd better move your cello back – no, I don't care if you do prefer it here in the middle, the viola has to sit here, it's not fair on him to have only the double bass for support back there. Yes, please move back, stop making such a fuss."

The cellist shrugged, patted the second violinist and, to her puzzlement, whispered, "I'm around if you need me."

After stowing his kit back at his normal seat and swapping the band parts around, back to the correct stands, he followed the rest of the orchestra into the corridor where the company dispensed tea and coffee to the players.

The second violinist was still in her seat, busy wiping excess rosin off her strings, but sensed something and looked to her left. Easing himself with a smirk into the viola's seat was her ex-husband.

"You!" she exploded, regardless of the curious stares of the public over the pit rail. "What are you doing in *my* theatre? What do I have to do to get rid of you? Who sent you?"

"Well, well, little one, just your little self as always. You haven't improved. Oh, by the way, I didn't think much of your bow technique in the first act. You're still not using your wrist correctly."

She fought back tears of frustration. She had a shrewd idea that all fixers in the area had known to avoid booking him and her together since their high-profile divorce, and players who knew their history would also avoid sending either as a dep if the other was playing. From what little she knew of him, she couldn't believe the normal viola would be so devious as to have set this up as a joke; he must simply have had no idea.

Collecting her dignity, she said quietly, "Well, I'm playing for the good of the show. I'm sorry if it isn't good enough for you."

She pointedly locked her violin case and took her part with her – she didn't trust him not to rub out her annotations, or detune her violin, while her back was turned – and went into the tea corridor. There, the leader and the cellist were gesticulating furiously until, upon seeing her, they turned away, embarrassed. The leader got out his mobile phone, while the cellist ambled up to the knot of people around the MD.

Act II opened with a tune shared by cello and first violins, with second violins and viola providing a harmonic scrub. Where on earth was he finding the subdivisions, it sounded like five semiquavers to the beat? Always when they differed, she had assumed she must be in the wrong, but she knew she had been playing well this week, and for the first time began to wonder.

Now for Giorgio's entrance, where there was an unwritten comma in the music that she and all the orchestra sensed together … except the viola jumped in mechanically with the subtlety of a clockwork carthorse. Then, at the end of Act II, the men's chorus entered a bar early, which the orchestra all seamlessly accommodated, except her ex. Was he trying to wreck the ensemble? No, she decided at last, it wasn't malice, it was that he really couldn't hold the rhythm or keep the place. Surely even the leader must hear how the ensemble was suffering. Thank goodness the singers were not letting themselves be put off.

She spent the second interval hiding in the Ladies, she

couldn't bear the risk that she might have to speak to her ex. But Act III was a torture. The opening Preludio is repeated, to symbolise Violetta's fate, and her ex failed to enter after his rest. Well, true, the regular viola did that at the band call, but that was for emotional reasons, not because of incompetence. Later, to contrast with Violetta's gloom, the off-stage chorus sings a cheerful but very difficult 'Mardi Gras' snatch, in the lead-up to which they need total accuracy from the orchestra. She cringed at the lack of accuracy from her ex.

Nor was he secure in the off-the-beat accompaniments, surely second nature to any viola, that viola and second violin play together so frequently in this opera. And when she thought they were safely home, he contrived to spoil the final cello-and-leader andantino duet, schmaltzy but effective, where Violetta seems to revive and lose her pain just before collapsing dead.

She began to wonder whether she couldn't learn to play the viola as well as he, whom she had once hero-worshipped. The viola was probably even more awkward and unwieldy than the violin, but she had overcome the violin pain barrier twenty years ago, and that must be a start.

There was still the Saturday evening performance to come. She had no idea how she would get through it with her ex sitting next to her trying all the time, deliberately or not, to put her off. It was so unfair that her most promising week ever in a pit should end on such a sour note. She readily agreed to join the cellist, the leader and another of the violinists for an Indian meal between the matinée and the evening house, feeling safe from her ex in a foursome.

She and the cellist tried to persuade the leader to revert to the unconventional seating for the evening performance, but the leader sternly said this topic was off-limits. After that, except that the leader kept leaving them to speak on his mobile phone, the conversation was pleasant and kept to safe subjects, such as the respective abilities of various composers to write sympathetically for strings. They awarded Verdi top marks for this *Traviata*.

After their leisurely if rather expensive dinner, the foursome returned to the theatre which, for the first time, had become an unpleasant place for her. The leader grumpily insisted they use the stage door, which meant she would not even pass her man-and-saxophone icon.

She forced herself into the pit which, until now, had been her favourite place on earth. She made herself look at the viola desk. But sitting at it was not her ex, it was her new friend from earlier that week! Overjoyed, she raced to him, tripped over an electric cable and landed headlong in his lap.

"Oh, am I glad to see you!" she exclaimed. "How come you're here?"

"My goodness, are you all right? They said there was some problem with my dep and I had to come back. They even squared it with the symphony orchestra I was supposed to be playing with tonight. All seems a bit dramatic to me."

"Oh, it's not a bit dramatic. It's simply saved my life. I want to learn the viola. Will you teach me?"

The MD

"*You* answer it," ordered my wife, who was up a step-stool taking down our Christmas decorations. "I bet it's someone wants you to do a show, it always is."

"Rubbish," I replied through the persistent ringing. "Everyone knows we're moving to Wales at Easter."

I picked up the phone. "Oh yes, I know that show," my wife heard me say, "we saw it only recently in the West End. ... Yes, I heard Fred's been picked as MD, bet he's pleased to be doing ... What, his company really said he had to do his year in their Moscow office or lose his job? ... Well, what's all that got to do with me?"

And so it came that I was appointed to replace Fred as Musical Director, halfway through the rehearsals for the British amateur première in March. It was an honour that some men would have killed for. I did say "men", not many women MDs around, don't know why not, the few that there are get good results. I wouldn't have accepted, but it was the producer himself who was asking me, and he's one of the best.

The producer told me he had already accepted some changes that Fred had recommended, inserting extra music between verses to cover on-stage business. Though I didn't agree with all the changes, I was stuck with them as the company were already rehearsing them.

Apart from putting aside some time to study the music, I had to attend not just the company's singing and choreography rehearsal on Tuesdays and the principals' rehearsal on Thursdays, but also some extra business-and-dialogue rehearsals on Fridays, because, as Fred had rightly found, this show had many places where the music had to follow actions and speech on stage.

Each week, I noticed how excellent the rehearsal accom-panist was, and I was pleased to discover that Fred had already booked him to do the week's run in the pit in March. The hired keyboard reductions that we were using were neatly handwritten and nicely laid out, except of course where we were having to splice in changes of our own.

It was suddenly busy at the office, so, for our move to Wales, my wife was having to clear out the household's accumulated junk single-handed, as she didn't fail to remind me in the few moments we had together.

"Ah," she said on one of the rare evenings I arrived home from work punctually, "you can help with clearing your wardrobe. You don't wear half ..."

"Not really this evening, I can't," I replied wearily. "I need a band, I've left it late enough already, I'll have to start phoning around right now."

Normally, I'd book my band as soon as I was appointed myself. Over the years, I'd got a good crew together, who knew how I worked. I could trust them not to let me down, even if they got offers of better jobs meanwhile. But by now, the best ones would already be committed, and if I expected them to honour *my* bookings, I couldn't ask them to break other engagements for my sake. And because I normally booked my players early, I didn't have (never needed) all that many spare names in my little black book. I'd have to ask other MDs to recommend some instrumentalists – they'd asked me for names often enough.

Any other show but this, you could be sure that most of your musicians had played it before. But this, being the amateur première, only the rehearsal accompanist had seen it and even his part would be quite different in the full orchestration, bound to be, as it called for *two* keyboard synthesisers. As the publishers hadn't released the parts yet, I'd need some confident accurate sight-readers.

I started with the reeds. I would need five stars. I soon realised I wasn't going to get them. Trying to fix a band is a good way of discovering what other musical activities are on. *Charlie Girl* was on the same week in the next county, and that took four saxophones out of circulation at a stroke.

So then I tried Ian. He was clear for the week except that he was playing the solo in Eric Coates's *Saxo Rhapsody* at a light music concert on the Saturday.

"No," I had to say, which I was to repeat to many others in my little black book, "this is the amateur première, it's the company's jubilee production, it's my last show, it's jolly awkward music by the look of it, I can't risk any deps, least of all on the Saturday."

I knew he'd be disappointed, he would dearly have wanted to play this show *and* the *Rhapsody*. The irony was that his sight-reading was so brilliant that he was one of the few I'd have accepted as a dep.

Try Joe next. His wife answers, tells me he's just agreed to play clarinet in *Pink Champagne* to replace the original clarinettist, who was poached to play sax in, guess what, *Charlie Girl*, except that as Joe's doing a Big Band on Saturday, he's put in Harry as a dep for that day. Just my rotten luck, Harry would have been my next call.

As light relief, I fixed a second keyboard, two guitarists and all my brass. The second-rank players all accepted with eagerness, positively toadying in their thanks at being asked. It was the better players, the ones I needed more, who whistled through their teeth, complained about their crowded diaries and quibbled about details.

Then a breakthrough. A cruise-shipping company had just gone bust. Within a few minutes of each other, two highly experienced chaps off one of the liners phoned me to say they'd just been paid off at Southampton and were available for any work, and would I please pass on the message to any other MDs. One was a percussionist, which was marvellous, and, even better, the other was a saxophonist.

So, eventually I did get my five reeds. They mostly didn't know each other, but I could take a chance on that as they were all experienced dance-band players and they would gel immediately.

Now for the strings. Problems, problems. This was a jazzy show, not normal string fare at all. I could foresee unrest from my string players not liking to play with keyboards, what with their different tuning; too bad, I couldn't worry about that now. Another problem was that strings who haven't played together seem to take an age to sound well. It was far too late to get the seven I needed from any pre-existing ensemble, so I just went for the best I knew.

Fourth violin was a difficult seat to fill, and, with some misgivings, I booked the principal second violin from the chamber orchestra I ran. She was a crisp economical player with a full tone and could read anything, but prim and inhibited. It always made me smile (inwardly) in rehearsals, how she would park her pencil not on the floor or on the music stand like anybody else, but poked through her bun.

Finally, my double bass. I've never really known why you have to have a double bass, it must be for appearance's sake. The instrument's big and unwieldy and can never be heard anyway. I could take all that if it weren't for the players of this ridiculous monstrosity, they all think they're so special that the world has to revolve around them. Well,

71 unsuccessful calls later, I decided to do without and to tell my bass guitar to turn up his amplifier.

Just when my wife had hoped I could make a start on packing my books, the producer came round to take me to view the theatre. I'd seen a play there but never been backstage. I'd never seen anything to rival it – newly painted, spacious, well-maintained, even a proper bandroom. The pit was enormous, with no junk or mess or obstructions. It was clean and well-kept. The band would love it. There was comfortably room for thirty if the budget would run to it.

"No," my producer shouted down from the stage, where he was inspecting some scenery-lifting mechanism, "you're being allowed 22 musicians, and that's generous" (which, in truth, it was).

The vast stage and cavernous wings bothered me. The producer knew the theatre, but even so I wondered whether ambition would get the better of him and tempt him to so fill the stage that scene changes will take twice as long as the provided music. I made a mental note to be prepared to repeat scene change music "till ready", and perhaps even have an emergency utility written out and ready on the music stands for the band to play instantly on my signal. I'd wait until the band parts came through, to orchestrate my utility the same as the nearest comparable number.

Except that the band parts never did come. I pestered the production secretary, the publishers, everybody. With only a couple of days to go, in desperation I collected two dozen vocal scores from the publisher's warehouse, in the hope that the band could vamp the tunes from those. We were actually setting up the bandcall itself, when a van pulled up and the driver brought the box of parts. In relief, I checked that the parts were all there and put them out on the stands. The van driver then departed with all those extra vocal scores.

Just moments later, the cellist came over and demanded to know, "How can we read this rubbish?"

Unlike my neat, well-spaced carefully bar-numbered piano reduction from which I'd been working, and I assumed all the music copying would be to the same standard, his part was hastily scrawled, with obvious evidence of cut-and-stick amendments.

His was one of the better parts, I soon found. And when we started to play, we found enormous discrepancies between the parts: reference letters in different places, different repeats and different numbers of bars. Some had song-introductions deleted from others, or shorter or longer endings. One part had the hit song in the wrong key.

In the middle of sorting this out, which the company couldn't understand and they were getting impatient, suddenly technicians and a presenter from the local radio station turned up, to record a few moments of the rehearsal and to interview the producer. I did recall being warned about this possibility, but had assumed it wouldn't actually happen because it was all "maybe" and "if their budget allows" and "if there's time left in their Arts slot". We had to shut windows which were letting in extraneous noise, we had to reposition singers, we had to find a song for which the band parts were in reasonable agreement, we had to make sure nobody in the band objected.

We did find a suitable duet, it recorded well, and our morale rose. By taking shortcuts, we rehearsed most of the music. Normally, when the band parts needed to be amended, I'd dictate the changes at the band call, on the basis that the musicians would understand their own pencilled writing and abbreviations more reliably than mine. No chance of that in the time allowed for the band call; I had to take the parts home and check them all. It took me all night. I then slept through the daytime and woke up just in time to get to the dress rehearsal.

I handed the parts out to the players as they arrived. Checking his part, my second keyboard player smoothed down the page and yelped in pain – he'd torn a finger on a staple that hadn't been properly bent over, that's how sloppily and hastily these parts had been prepared. Someone had a roll of heavy-duty sticky tape and I applied it down the centrefold of every one of the parts, to avoid a repetition. Yet another chore for an MD.

At the dress rehearsal, as I had hoped, the orchestra were bowled over by the pit. None had played in this one before, and the real live stage door keeper was a novelty to many of them. However, the playing was pedestrian except from the reeds and percussion, who'd got the mood of the show straight away. As I had foreseen, Miss Prim played correctly but vaguely disapprovingly and with no sense of swing at all. The cellist behind her was tickling his way through his part, no feeling of a coherent bass line. The bass guitar was good but followed his own agenda, not my beat. I began to regret having no double bass but I was stuck with that now.

During the dialogue, as traditional, the musicians craned their necks and stood up to see the stage. I didn't worry – musicians have this sixth sense when a song is imminent. Although I do remember once they got it wrong; it was the dialogue preceding the Septet in *Rose of Persia*, and my orchestra reckoned they were safe as long as the number of actors on stage wasn't exactly seven, but there were so many rapid-fire entrances and exits they lost count ...

Well, even standing and craning necks, *this* pit was too low for any of my band to see any of the stage. They could only pick up the mood of the show from hearing the dialogue, which wasn't flowing well. Nor was the music. Even after I'd checked the mike for each instrument myself, the orchestral sound balance was atrocious, but the theatre staff kept assuring me that they would have set up the mixer correctly by the opening night.

Dressed in all-black as I had ordered, the band looked seriously ready for action on opening night. I climbed onto my high conductor's stool and was happy to see that the hydraulic pit had been left at exactly the right height for me just to see the stage. I knew the actors could see me regardless, through a cctv system with on-stage monitors mounted just out of the audience's sight; I had a miniature screen next to me showing the same image.

The band looked up at me, waiting for the green light and then my downbeat. Again, the fawning looks of nervous respect at me, the infallible all-powerful MD.

Could they guess that I was much more nervous? My bad luck that the parts were in such a mess, my judgment whether we had enough scene-change music. My choice to accept the show. My choice of musicians, my gamble that they could sight-read this, which I knew they couldn't have seen before. Whatever happened, it was down to me. The musicians would survive a flop and continue to get work in future, but I'd be remembered and blacklisted. If I took up MD'ing again in Wales, not that I was meaning to but it gets in the blood, horror stories of my flop would be bound to reach the selection committees, probably magnified in the telling.

The green light flashing on my music stand brought me back to reality. Go! I flick my left hand in time to warn them of the brisk upbeat tempo to come, and with my right I beat out the opening chords. Wow, not only do my musicians *look* serious, they *are*. They really used the dress rehearsal to learn. Precise playing, yet also capturing the mood, from the first moment. Against all the odds, and reading this flydirt music, made worse by my late-night corrections, these fine but individualistic musicians hailing from all sorts of musical styles had gelled.

Even Miss Prim let her hair down, in both senses. In a silly number where the hero fantasises about tap dancing in the court of Louis XIV, a quartet of female beatniks with long silver-tinsel wigs joins in his dance. Their wigs were shaking like waterfalls in rhythm and Miss Prim's equally long hair was shaking, exactly against the rhythm, as she threw herself into the syncopations. The audience couldn't see the band and the band couldn't see the stage; in the whole theatre, only I, and the lads in the lighting box, could see all of this remarkable picture.

But somebody had seen some of it. At the interval, the first trumpet, a bruisingly self-confident young fellow, crossed the invisible line in the bandroom separating the burgers and six-packs from the vegetarian sandwiches and herbal teabags, to chat to the transformed Miss Prim.

On Wednesday morning I got a call from the viola. He told me he'd sprained his wrist, but hoped to be OK by tomorrow, Thursday. Shortly afterwards, the first trumpet called. He told me his lip was bruised from someone accidentally flinging a door open in his face. He also thought he'd be fit to play by Thursday.

Determined to avoid introducing new players, and as it would be just for the one night, I decided to dispense with the viola and get the lads on the sound desk to turn up the cello mike. Blissfully, I didn't then know that it had in fact fused and the computer driving the mixing board wouldn't accept any sounds coming in on that channel.

I was more worried about the trumpet; I didn't want to re-orchestrate all the brass for just one performance, so I simply promoted the second trumpet to first. He was a steady chap, ran a youth band, incredibly thin lips for a brass player, didn't play with that brash edge of joyful exhibitionism that you want in a first trumpet for this sort of show. I just had to hope that he would get the message off his answering machine in time to get to the theatre early enough to read through the part, to psyche himself up for some bright playing.

As I arrived at the theatre that evening, Miss Prim was looking severer than ever and avoided me. On my way in, the stage-door-keeper handed me a newspaper cutting. Not a first-night review as I'd expected, but a news item about a fight in the multi-storey car park.

Eventually I pieced it all together. The viola had had designs on Miss Prim, after all she was sitting right next to him in the pit. He was so outraged on spotting her sitting in the first trumpet's car at the end of the previous night's performance that he rammed the car and pulled the trumpeter out. In the ensuing punch-up, they sustained the injuries they'd told me of. I couldn't believe violas had such strong feelings about anything; my opinion of them went up.

The newspaper review was probably pinned up somewhere backstage, but with all this distraction I forgot to look for it and, if I *had* thought, I'd have preferred not to know. The music was a success but the production as a whole had to be a flop, mainly because the anti-heroine was frankly unbelievable. The actress was way over the top on a character which was already over the top. Vain, envious, malicious, contemptuous, with an out-of-character song complaining that she couldn't get her man and, at the end, a hysterical outburst bewailing that she can't sing, when she's spent the whole show boasting about her abilities. The romantic heroine was colourless next to her. *I* was lucky, what the opening night's audience had cheered (and how!) was the dancing and music.

Wednesday was a disaster. I'd brought the wrong spectacles and kept misreading the score. I'd asked the second keyboard player to fill in any missing cues that the viola or second trumpet should have played, but he got confused and muddled it all up. His ripped finger didn't help, and he said that my brown tape, though appreciated (what a boot-licker), was pulling the pages shut and they wouldn't lie properly open on the stand. The hero forgot his lines in the hit song. The scene-changes, which had been quite fast on opening night, were noisy and slow.

At one point, the percussionist had to overturn a tray full of rivets and bolts onto another metal tray, on my signal, to coincide with the anti-heroine supposedly throwing a tray of crockery off a balcony (in reality, passing it to a stagehand out of sight). My percussionist completely missed the moment, and then, when reaching for his wire brushes ready for a love duet, leaned clumsily and set off the whole clattering noise just as the romantic interest was heightening. At the end of the evening, I found him in his car in the car park, staring straight ahead expressionlessly. I tapped on the windscreen to say words of consolation, at which he looked fixedly away.

Thursday, back to my full complement of players. I needed to prevent any renewed outbreaks of Tuesday's gross indiscipline. I couldn't issue the ultimate threat, to cross their names out of my book, as they knew I was retiring. Instead, I had to let it be known that I was docking people who missed a night for whatever reason. It seemed to clear the air, and Thursday did go better. The dance routines had come alive, not that my musicians would see those, but they should sense from the applause that something was going well.

In any case, I could tell they were beginning to relax. During the dialogues, each was slouching in his own characteristic way. The third violin would stand his fiddle upright on his lap and rest his chin on the scroll, the cellist was resting his bow against his shoulder, the percussionist was reading, I blush to guess what, on his music stand.

On Friday, recovered from being the centre of such unwelcome excitement, Miss Prim was back to her amazing new uninhibited self, fairly safe now from extra-musical intervention. Those lads in the lighting-and-technicals box obviously liked looking at her too, because I noticed that evening, and I'm sure it hadn't been there before, a pencil-beam of light from the auditorium ceiling was trained straight down onto her; only the lighting lads could possibly have done it. When I tackled them about it at the interval, perhaps not as diplomatically as I might have done, they counter-attacked, claiming that my cellist had tapped the cello-stand mike to hear if it was live, which had not only wrecked it but had also blown the feed into the mixing desk.

After that irritation, Friday's show was quite respectable in all departments. The actors' timing was good, their voice projection had adjusted to the size of the theatre, all the scenes with throwing things, catching things and bumping into each other went correctly, and the anti-heroine-throws-crockery-from-balcony scene was spot-on, my percussionist being so accurate that I could even hold off so that the clatter was delayed, giving the impression that the balcony was several storeys up. But I still didn't recognise a West-End smash-hit in this production.

During the playout, there suddenly appeared on my cctv screen a cartoon film of a mad musician. A personal message from the lighting box, I suppose.

Saturday, the last night, was unbelievable. My musicians were miraculously accurate, well, I'd gone for the best so they should have been, illegible music regardless. The lighting, the slick scene-changing, the sound effects all going right. What really made it was the anti-heroine. She'd at last got the measure of her part. All the little touches of malice and venom were pitched to be believable and well-relieved by her occasional moments of frankness and insight into her shortcomings. I realised I'd never seen such a well-written fully developed anti-heroine part. The audience were practically hissing her, gasping at every stratagem that she was employing to discredit the romantic heroine. Even the male lead, excellent tap-dancer as he had to be, and well applauded for that, was a nobody next to this bravura performance.

The applause at the end came across in waves that you could almost feel. Even the pit was being cheered. I bowed from the pit – there wasn't time to go round and up onto the stage, which in this theatre was about half a mile of corridors away.

After umpteen curtain calls, I started the playout. I could feel the enthusiasm of the audience and its reluctance to leave the theatre while any part of the production was still alive in it. Ineluctably, we reached the last note of the playout. I savoured the moment. I held the last chord, while my mind replayed my entire conducting career in fast-forward. The reeds were going purple in the face from holding the last note. The strings were panting from the exhaustion of scrubbing with their bows. The percussionist was deafening even himself.

Reluctantly, I gave my baton the last flick to end the last note of my last show.

I had given almost every spare hour of my life to music, and the last three months of it to this. In my wildest imaginings, I never dreamt that it would be received so triumphantly. What a high note on which to retire.

And yet, next week, next year, who would remember the show, or even remember me?

The Double Bass Player

"Nothing ever happens in your silly pit, does it. I wish you'd stay at home rather than be out every evening."

Her boyfriend's words rang in her ears as she drove off after Sunday lunch to the venue for *No, No, Nanette*. Her annoyance faded as she concentrated on finding her way to the theatre, which was in a distant suburb she had never visited before.

As she eventually steered her battered estate car into the theatre's front car park, the magnificence of the building took her breath away. It doubled as the local Town Hall, built in the days when municipal pride was considered a virtue and not something shameful. The entrance foyer led to a splendid art deco staircase up to the theatre auditorium. That she even noticed this was a tribute to the architect, as her interest in buildings was usually restricted to whether the doors would let her double bass through, without swinging shut and hitting it.

The auditorium was even more impressive, with thick carpeting, high-quality wood panelling, and fine concealed lighting. When new in the 1930s, it must have been sensational.

Like a pack animal shaking off its load, she slid the double bass off her shoulder and put down her stool. She strolled around, admiring the theatre. When she reached the pit rail, to inspect her place of work for the coming week, she could see where the money had run out. The pit was plain and shabby with a rough-sawn planked floor, and was about four feet down. It extended right and left under the auditorium floor, she could not see how far. It would be her job to produce cheerful music in this sad pit.

As the other musicians began to arrive, she recognised only one, and it was a surprise: a cellist from her po-faced symphony orchestra. She had no idea he did shows.

The band call was to be held in a small clear area at the back of the auditorium itself, and helpers from the operatic company were putting out chairs and music stands. The stands were an old-fashioned type; only one in the set would extend tall enough. If she was lucky it would have a distinguishing mark painted on it, but not this time. Once she had found it, however, she would never have to fuss and shuffle to sight the beat, she on her high stool could always see everything.

"Hello one and all," said the MD to start the band call, "whatever you do this week, put your car in the front car park. Anywhere else, and it might vanish. Though it's not as bad as it was, because the estate where the lads came from has been demolished. So don't bother using the stage door round the back, just come in the front way. You can only get into the pit through the gate in the front rail anyway."

She opened her band part, which contained fewer pages of music to play, and more of it pizzicato, than in any other show she could remember. Typical of double bass parts for shows, it was a quarter the thickness of the first violin part, and also typical of double bass parts for shows, its hardest number was the Overture, after which there was little to challenge her technically.

As she played through it, she was rather disappointed by the music itself, with little of interest, neither the scrunchy harmonies of say *Carousel* nor the four-square rhythms of *Gondoliers* (with its second-act chorus having the words which so amused her, "Proclaim their Graces, O ye double basses"). Some of the numbers had intermediate titles, such as 'Two Beat Jazz' written in spidery writing at a double bar halfway through no.6, but she wondered why, as she could see no change in the character of the music at those points.

She had so little problem in sight-reading her part that she feared that, as the week went on, she would lose her place through plain inattention. Perhaps her boy friend was right about the boredom and strain of the pit and she should give it up after this week.

The next evening, before the start of the dress rehearsal, she decided to note everything that happened this week, to see if it was really so uneventful. When she stepped down into this pit for the first time, she found it was so deep, with no view at all (even for her) of the stage or the auditorium, that her boy friend's odds looked good. The pit had deep layers of dust and fluff. A rusty radiator right next to her position emitted heat that would surely become intolerable later in the week.

Worse was to come. The auditorium floor had been extended over both ends of the pit, converting them into a pair of dark caves, too low to stand up in. A grand piano was incongruously trapped half-way into the cave on the strings' side, leaving the string section very tight for space.

The cellist continually got in her way as he leaned into his bag to slurp coffee from his flask or munch a snack. In contrast to his impeccable behaviour in her dead-serious orchestra, he was quite the fidgetiest and most distracting cellist she had ever had the misfortune to share a pit with. The discipline on him of being visible to audience or actors was totally absent. Her earlier pleasure at recognising him soon evaporated.

The double bass player found the inside of the grand piano to be a convenient receptacle for her rosin, her duster, her sandwiches, her bow, her sweets, her mute, her pencil, her spectacles and her other bits and pieces. These included a roll of surgical tape, with which she bound her pizzicato finger, which was already raw from just the band call. The pianist accepted her invasion of his instrument with patient good humour.

He needed patient good humour; he had to play in unspeakably troglodytic conditions well inside the cave, its darkness relieved only by his single music-stand light. But the cave would be ideal for leaving her double bass overnight, completely out of sight. At the end of the dress rehearsal, the cellist decided he would do the same in case he might be detained late at his office the next evening; he could then go direct to the theatre without having to deviate via his home to collect his cello.

He snuggled his cello up to her double bass and asked her, "When we come back tomorrow evening, do you think we'll find they've given birth to a viola?"

"No," she replied severely, having just bumped her head on the low ceiling, "more likely matchwood."

When she arrived home, her boyfriend greeted her: "Thank goodness you've left your double bass there. I hate it, I hate its brooding presence in this flat, it's so huge it dominates everything. At least your cello wasn't always in the way, I don't know what possessed you to give it up for the double bass."

Sometimes she wondered why herself. And maybe her boyfriend had a point. The next evening, from the theatre, she phoned her widowed aunt, who lived not far away.

"Why, bless you," replied her aunt, "of course you can leave your double bass here. When your dear uncle died, I converted his study into a second guest bedroom but I've never needed it, so your double bass could easily go there. And your stool."

On Tuesday, the opening night, she noticed that after the overture and opening number, there was a good quarter-hour's dialogue. She welcomed this: if her ageing car broke down and delayed her even quite substantially, she would probably still miss only those two numbers.

She was amused to hear the actor playing the young lawyer succumb to opening night nerves and say, "I do like this job; it's *dangerous* without being too *exciting*," when it should have been the other way round.

She then concentrated on her playing until a dance sequence 'Peach on the Beach,' in which a flamboyantly huge beach ball floated gracefully off the stage and sank slowly into the pit. When a violinist deflected it out of his way with his bow, it looped gently towards her and touched the hot lamp housing of her music stand. It burst with a loud pop, and a singed shred of it blew into her hair.

Musically, however, her first impression was confirmed; her part was unexciting even by the modest standards of double bass parts. Perhaps that actor had been right after all to say "dangerous without being too exciting."

As she crossed the backstage obstacle course to the Ladies during the interval, she overheard a fierce argument from inside the men's changing room: the MD was hotly defending his orchestra against accusations from the singers of missing cue notes.

The company was having technical problems too. One was the telephone which failed to ring but nonetheless had to be "answered" by the actor, making a nonsense of the scene. Another was the intrusive creaking noise made by the spotlights as they cooled, and this became worse each night, defeating the orchestra's best efforts to achieve a poignant atmosphere in the quiet chords closing the Tea For Two Dance.

Before Wednesday's start, the MD spoke to various players asking them to pencil in some extra notes. They glumly complied, realising that these were the notes which should have been played by musicians who, to save money, had been omitted from this week's band. The double bass player was ready on principle to refuse to play extra notes which somebody else ought to have been employed to play, but it never came to that, because the MD didn't ask her. Only the cellist jumped up and down with tasteless glee at being given some bassoon snatches to play, shouting, "My big solo, at last, my big solo!"

With these changes, the Wednesday performance proceeded. It turned out that the other musicians had also noticed the long dialogue after the first song; out of bravado, the wind and percussion had brought in take-away burgers-and-chips to eat during this dialogue, but they had not bargained on the persistence of the aroma and they did not repeat the treat. After that night, there was still always a flurry of activity at this point as the musicians got out their magazines or caught up with their correspondence.

As on the opening night, she heard raucous laughter and applause at one point, and kneeled on her high stool to try to see what was so amusing. In vain. She made a note in her part to peer up earlier the next night. She was starting to feel happier with this show; she was coming to see that the arranger had not been unkind to the double bass. She began to recognise places where her contribution was important, indeed essential. One was that section marked 'Two Beat Jazz' in no.6, another was 'Early Blues' in no.11. Other important places were the 'Old Time Fun' in no.17, two separate Dixieland Gallops in no.18 and the 'Two-Beat Groove' in no.22. She always looked forward to these.

Little routines started to establish themselves. Uncle Jimmy, who had to play the banjo on-stage but cheerfully admitted he was tone-deaf, would come to the pit rail for his nightly tune-up. The double bass player would reach up and tune his banjo for him; the pity was that when the actor's time came to strum it, it had already gone out of tune.

The pit was accumulating its usual detritus – empty lager cans, bits of a clothes peg that had broken while in use to stop pages on someone's part from flopping over, a half-eaten sandwich abandoned on the floor ...

On Thursday, she kneeled up where she had reminded herself on her band part to do so. On stage, she saw a vacuum cleaner roll unaided from the wings towards the maid. The maid commanded the vacuum cleaner to go away, and it did, again unaided. It was a clever and very funny effect, fully deserving the laughter it earned.

At the interval, she looked up to see an admiring crowd of children peering down over the pit rail. The sheer size of her double bass impressed them and they asked to hear it. She started to play 'The Elephant' from the Carnival of the Animals, but had to stop after a few bars because, to her shame, she had forgotten it. The children didn't seem to mind, and showed a lively and well-informed interest in the pit, being able to name the instruments they saw. She was delighted. *They* would not grow up to steal cars, and maybe some of them would in due time themselves create live music in pits, keeping the craft alive for another generation. At the end of that evening, she went home quite happy. Until her boyfriend greeted her.

"Your cello was OK except for all the time it took up, but your double bass is something else. Why, even the strings, when you get them out of their packet, they're not musical-looking, they remind me of ship's hawsers."

How could she explain to someone who had never done it? Things didn't happen in pits, she and her double bass *made* them happen. Perched on her stool, she would survey the whole pit orchestra spread out in front of her. She provided the carpet of sound for the rest to perform on. And when it came to tempo changes in the middle of numbers, it was she who felt like the driver, moving the music on or reining it back.

"It's not even as if you get any tunes to play, on your double bass," he continued to taunt her.

How could he ever understand the feeling at those moments every evening, when the music would reach the friendly words written in spidery writing on her band part – 'Two-Beat Groove' – at which the rest of the orchestra would fall silent, leaving her alone with two or three reeds and percussion to play the dances. This was her world, the feeling of power providing the harmonic floor and the rhythm, she held it together and pushed it along. Without her, she knew it would all fall apart.

After a couple of nights, this band-within-a-band had started to feel like a unit in its own right. It was good, but still not 100%. While her boyfriend continued to air his opinions, she formed an idea.

The next night, Friday, pausing at home only to change into

regulation black, write a note to the milkman, put her boyfriend's meal into the oven, feed his dog and shovel some microwaved food down her own throat, she rushed to the theatre. The cellist, arriving soon afterwards, curse him, saw her kneeling on the floor of the pit, ear flat on the ground, tapping, crawling a few inches and tapping again. He laughed at her undignified posture and the dust all over her clothes. Laugh your head off, she thought, I've found the resonant spot at last. She pulled the rubber bung off the endpin of her double bass and planted the bare metal endpin on the floor at that spot.

Come the first dance, her pizzicato rang solidly round the pit as never before, the planked floor acting as a huge soundboard. The rest of the band-within-a-band responded. Bouncing off her rock-steady confident bass line with its bright rising harmonies, the dance resounded thrillingly round the pit; it no longer *sounded* like Dixieland, it *was* Dixieland. Every dance sounded better than the last. Once sure that the tempo was right for the dancers, the MD even stopped conducting for the 64 bars of each dance sequence, he knew he was only in the way of the inspiration around him.

This is what it was all about, a handful of craftsman soloists creating from nothing a marvellous infectious pulsating excitement. From her lordly vantage point, she looked round at the rough-sawn planking, the dust, the litter, the dog-eared magazines, the broken clothes peg, the dried-up half-eaten sandwich – she had brought this sad pit to life!

In the interval, the cellist timidly asked whether he could join her in playing the bass line in the dances.

"No you can't," she beamed happily. "You've got lots of scrumptious solos of your own to wallow in."

"Solos? In *No No Nanette?*" replied the cellist, hurt. "You're joking. There's nothing in this part, nothing to compare with your dances."

"Well, you still can't."

"All right, can I try out your double bass?"

"Yes, if you let me try out your cello."

The cellist climbed gingerly up her stool and produced only a pitiful groan from her instrument. Subdued, he watched as she picked up his cello, pretending unfamiliarity. She opened his part 'by chance' at a flourish from the overture that he had never quite mastered. She tossed off the flourish perfectly.

Deflated, he behaved quite well after that, even playing with a little care. He still went into double speed at one point, at which she took pity on him. To save him from the ignominious domino to which he was heading, she hit his shoulder with her bow.

"Thanks, but couldn't you have warned me *before* I went wrong?"

"Ah, I charge extra for telepathy," she replied.

The prompt, sitting directly in front of the MD, had never had to intervene all week, and announced (which, in view of the depth of the pit, would have been the more sensible option in the first place) that she would prompt from the wings on the last night.

For already the next night was Saturday, the closing night. The leader had appointed a deputy for this night, who had to come in cold and sight-read a show which had evolved subtly over the week beyond the bare notes on the staves. There was some muttering about this from the other musicians, but the double bass player knew who could rescue any wrong rhythm or harmony. Herself.

The vacuum cleaner scene earned exceptionally raucous laughter, and she realised why, when, some guide-wire having snapped, the vacuum cleaner appeared at the edge of the pit, wobbled and fell in, plumb in the middle, into the one vacant spot. The audience, and tonight's leader, thought it was part of the act. The regular musicians knew otherwise and thought of the prompt's lucky escape. When they had recovered from their shock, the cellist whispered to the double bass player that they could have done with a vacuum cleaner in this dusty pit earlier in the week.

The pianist, though personally never in danger, being protected by the low ceiling, was still in a trance when Flora came to speak her line "I feel it right here," the cue for music no.11 'The Three Happies.'

Taking her band part off the stand, the double bass player waved it about in his line-of-sight, which was enough to jerk him back to reality and to start no.11 as a reflex reaction. In the rush to get herself re-organised to play, she caught her bow between the vertical sections of the cast-iron radiator, whereupon the cellist wrestled it free for her, not without an embarrassing clatter. The MD cast a grateful look at the double bass for having rescued the situation.

But her real reward would come in a moment, later in that number, at the 'Early Blues.' This dance went like a dream, with herself providing the foundation for a few reeds in glorious American blues. And the following dances, in both Acts, went better and better, with a brilliant vivacity that outshone even Friday's triumph. At the beginning of the week, she still hadn't known that music-making could ever be like this. While doing those dances, she was king of the universe. *Now* she knew why she had migrated to the double bass.

At the end of the playout, she was astonished to see audience pressing three-deep against the pit rail applauding and waving in appreciation. All this for a pit orchestra they hadn't even been able to see. There was warm hand-shaking and mutual back-slapping before the orchestra dispersed.

She made a detour to drop off her double bass at her aunt's, and then continued home.

Her boyfriend completely failed to notice the absence of the double bass and simply greeted her, "You're later than ever tonight! You can't possibly get anything out of spending all that time in a poky pit. You'd be better off staying at home with me."

"Is that so?" she said with icy calm, as she prepared to pack her bags and leave him.

The Oboist

So much depended on this booking, the first she had ever won by her own efforts.

Until now, she had lived in the shadow of her elder sister, an accomplished bassoonist, who had protectively insisted that anyone wanting herself on the bassoon had to have Little Sister to play oboe. The elder sister was popular and successful at everything she wanted – jobs, music, men – and now she had perished in a car crash.

Little Sister was suddenly left to make her own way. Little Sister was neither a music-college student nor a music teacher at a school, who are in the gossip circles about forthcoming shows and other similar work. But by making herself known, playing in amateur orchestras, chamber groups and anywhere she could find, she had at last secured this one-week booking in the pit orchestra for *South Pacific*.

Her letter, confirming the telephone call, told her that she was being engaged by the Metropolitan Bank Dramatic Club, that the run was at the Metropolitan Bank's Social Club Theatre from Tuesday to Saturday, with no matinée, that the dress rehearsal was on Monday at the theatre, nothing unusual in any of that, and that the band call would take place on Sunday morning, not at the theatre, but in the Metropolitan Bank's head office in the City. Well, that was no problem for her, carrying an oboe, but she pitied the percussionist who would have to lug his gear to the City and then take it all away again to the theatre in the suburbs.

It was a brilliant crisp Sunday morning when she emerged onto the street from the almost deserted underground station. She found to her surprise that the City was nearly as busy as on a weekday, with the absence of cars and taxis more than compensated by flotillas of builders' lorries and computer servicing vans. So much for the advice peddled by tourist guides to London, to visit the City on Sunday morning as being the quietest time.

She made her way to the Bank head office, and found herself standing in a Victorian marble reception hall which would not have disgraced a royal palace. However, as more and more musicians struggled in with their assorted cases and bags, the stately dignified hall soon took on the sordid look of an airline check-in.

Some of the arriving musicians exchanged greetings, and she gathered that a few had been in a show together the previous night, not twelve hours ago. She could not recognise anybody. Never mind, she would know everyone well enough by the end of the week.

Security staff eventually appeared and ushered everybody through the hall to a large goods lift at the back of the building. In shifts, the orchestra was conveyed to a canteen, which was being pressed into service as the rehearsal room. Some of the workmen with which the City was swarming this Sunday morning were evidently at work in this very bank, as a radio somewhere near the canteen blared out the latest hits.

"Sorry about the sound effects," said the MD, "but let's get on. Glad to see you all today. We'll be without a viola today and we'll be without our regular Nelly Forbush tomorrow," (at which someone, obviously cast as Nelly, bowed slightly), "because she's addressing an inter-governmental finance conference in Frankfurt tomorrow. Right then, I'll take the overture as written, starting in four, one beat for nothing then the upbeat."

Instantly, the air was filled with the Bali-Hai theme, and without the spacious volume and soft furnishings of a theatre, the sound thundered deafeningly round the canteen. To add to the noise, the many nearby City churches all started to chime the hour. Through all this, the oboist could still hear how the overture presented the many tuneful melodies of *South Pacific*. The musical exhilaration was infectious as the orchestra romped to the end of the overture.

The old hands in the orchestra probably thought nothing, but she wondered again at the small miracle that a group of mostly total strangers could come together, sit reading dots on a page which they had never seen before, or at least not recently, and, first time, produce such a magnificent sound. Unexpectedly, loud applause and cheering was heard from the hidden workmen. It must have been genuine, their blaring radio had stopped. What a promising start to her first week out of the wilderness!

The next evening, she arrived at the bank's Social Club in the suburbs for the dress rehearsal. Being early, she wandered round the building and marvelled at the lavish sporting and recreational facilities, very different from the notions she had of staff cuts and economies in the banking world. The posters on the notice board revealed that there was even a staff symphony orchestra which met here every week, and she smiled at the thought that she, not they, was being employed for this show.

Except for the fact that the "bandroom" was in reality a concrete corridor full of junk, the theatre inside this social complex turned out to have every last feature, including, as she was to see, a hydraulic height-adjustable pit. Only when all the orchestra were aboard would the stage manager close the safety doors and raise the pit to the appropriate level. Latecoming bandsmen would miss a whole act, but on the other hand the brass players wouldn't be able to sneak out for a drink between their numbers. Yes, she thought, it was all right being a brass player, often *tacet* throughout several consecutive songs, plenty of time to nip out to the bar.

Then again, she reminded herself of the embarrassing occasion in *Brigadoon*, when she lost count in a run of tacets. She came in boldly on what she thought was her next number, a celebratory march, when they had in fact reached only the previous number, an atmospheric interlude representing mysterious voices from another world.

Although the *South Pacific* dress rehearsal was indifferent, the show began to come to life as the week went on – the singers gained pace and confidence and the bandsmen began to toss off those runs and ornaments that had never fitted quite properly before.

By the Friday night, the orchestra was playing as a well-oiled machine until, in the second Act, a dull twang resonated round the pit. The co-leader first-violinist's E string had broken. While the leader carried on playing, his desk-partner the co-leader set to, as quietly and quickly as possible, to remove the broken halves of string, and fetched a new string out of his violin case lying by his chair.

Hampered by the poor light in the pit, he became so absorbed in trying to thread the new string through the hole in his peg that he failed to notice his leader reaching the end of the page.

Not used to turning his own pages, the leader failed to turn in time, and then clumsily turned two pages together. In this way he completely missed his solo, a snatch of six notes from the 'Some Enchanted Evening' theme, immediately preceding Nelly Forbush's song 'When You Find Your True Love.'

As the orchestra realised that this vital cue had been omitted, a sense of alarm flashed around the pit – what would happen, how to redeem this collapse?

In a recklessness brought on by the collective fright and indecision, the oboist, without really stopping to think, played the six notes by ear. The moment was saved and the performance got back on the rails again.

At the end, she saw the leader peering at her round the music stands separating them. She waited for the inevitable dressing-down.

"Jolly good," he said, to her surprise and relief, "just as well someone's awake down here. Tell you what, it sounded so good on the oboe, why don't you do it tomorrow too."

On the Saturday, in the interval between the Acts, she vaguely remembered she needed something from her coat pocket in the bandroom. On arriving there, she found the MD was treating his band to cakes, an unusual and welcome gesture, but not much help to her. While the string and brass players tucked in eagerly, and the flautist muttered that he could probably risk one cake without upsetting his breath control, the oboist and the bassoonist nodded at each other knowingly. A stray cake crumb could so easily find its way into the reed and block it at the most inopportune moment.

Just then, the MD opened a box of chocolates, much more up her street, even if the desiccated coconut centres weren't what she'd expected. In a haze of well-being, the band eventually filtered back into the pit for the second Act.

As the second Act got under way, her reed, which had been getting sweeter and more responsive all week, gave ominous signs of imminent collapse. She was having to blow that bit harder to get any sound at all, and the reed was locking up completely at not much higher pressure.

This problem came to a head during the 'Morse code' sequence, scene-setting music where the orchestra, in particular the oboe, mimics the ether full of competing military radio messages. In that sequence, a few dots or dashes fluffed or omitted by the oboe weren't noticeable, but she was dreading the imminent violin solo, which tonight was her solo. She really ought to change reeds now.

She had one in just the right condition, second from the right in her spares case. She reached into her oddments bag for her spares case. But her spares case wasn't there. Yes, that was what she had meant to collect from her coat pocket until she was distracted by the cakes and chocolate. With luck, she'd just have time to dash out and fetch it now.

Ha! Of course, there was no way out of this pit!

Sheer panic seized her at the thought of continuing with her present dying reed. Her mouth, already dry enough from the coconut centres, went as parched as sandpaper. She picked up the eggcup which she used to park her reed and swilled the few drops of water in it around her mouth. It didn't help at all, and now she had nothing left to keep the reed wet. She couldn't even go out to the Ladies to get water.

Her whispered message asking for a cup of water went along the line unanswered, until it reached the percussionist. Somewhat misunderstanding, he gravely poured out a cup of coffee from his flask and passed it back along the line. Meanwhile, she opened her tool box, a child's enamelled toy treasure chest. She surveyed it helplessly; it was full of fine wire, blades, plaques, scrapers and some contrivances of her own invention, but there was nothing in it to solve the present circumstance.

And the hot coffee which now arrived – fancy trying to wet her mouth with that! Or should she soak the reed in it? No, the milk in the coffee would surely clog it up. Whatever she did, disaster stared her in the face, followed by shame and ridicule.

Why on earth did she entrust her career to a stupid paper-thin piece of rotting cane, when she could have settled for something much more safe and sedate, such as sky-diving?

She took a measured gulp of coffee, which wetted her mouth a bit. If only her mouth were as damp as her sweating palms. She waited and watched for the fateful downbeat, as if it were a descending guillotine.

A fair pressure, not too much … tongue, and the first note

rang out true and pure. The next four notes, which were all within three semitones, emerged fractionally hesitantly, but adequately. Now for the last note of the six, a perfect fifth lower, and supposed to be on the weak beat.

The last note refused. Try a bit harder. Surely it wouldn't... Yes, that reed was now locking up under *too much* pressure. OK, ease off my girl, try again gently – but not too gently or nothing will come – attack it just so – nip a bit harder – oh, just forget that your lip's already bleeding – brace yourself – you know you can do it – tongue -

... at last, it seemed like ages, but it all really took only a moment, the reed exploded into life. The sixth note was heard, a bit sour, a bit off-key, and a bit late, but the phrase was completed. Relief flooded over her. She offered silent thanks to all her years' playing experience, which had seen her through this emergency.

From then to the end of the show, only a few minutes, she succeeded by some miracle in coaxing most of the oboe line out of the reed. She felt triumphant.

At the end, when the applause was finishing and instead of the playout music, the president of the bank took to the stage to make a speech congratulating the participants. The pit hydraulics whirred into action, and the Musical Director preened himself ready to take a bow. He made signs that he would bring the orchestra to their feet when, for the first time all week, the pit would rise high enough for the audience to see them.

But instead of rising, the pit was sinking. The hydraulics were lowering the pit to the exit level! So, the end-of-run anti-climax that used to grip her, usually somewhere on her journey home, came forcibly earlier, reinforced this time by the famine of the empty diary. The usual cheery remarks that the oboist was used to hearing, as bandsmen reflected on a job well done, simply didn't happen. As she listlessly dismantled her oboe and mopped it through, wishing the show could have gone on another few nights, she became aware of the leader standing next to her.

"Say, that was game of you," he said to her. "Reed trouble? And you never said. Well, look, I know it's a terrific cheek of me at such short notice, but I've fixed a band to do *My Fair Lady*, and I've just had a text message that my oboist can't do it. Thing is, the band call's tomorrow afternoon. Is there absolutely any chance at all you could do the whole week for me? Please?"

The Bassoonist

As he carried his bassoon case into the theatre on this dull Sunday afternoon, he felt he was coming home. Over the years, he had come to be the regular bassoonist for most of the amateur operatic companies which used this theatre, and, of those companies, this week's was his favourite.

The orchestra used by this company hardly varied from year to year, and was the nearest thing he had to a family. He would commiserate with one musician who had missed promotion at work, and he would rejoice with another whose daughter had gained a university place. He would follow all their families' fortunes with interest.

As usual, the band call was in the theatre bar, the bar itself being shuttered, and as the musicians – his "family" – arrived one by one, they would exchange their latest news. The horn player's son, whom the bassoonist remembered being born, had just passed his motorbike test. The bassoonist noticed only one new face in this week's orchestra – this suited him; he liked stability.

The show was My Fair Lady, which he enjoyed, having played it a number of times for other companies. Many of this orchestra, however, were having to sight-read it.

The company's singers had rehearsed their songs for six months, with a piano. Today was their first encounter with their orchestra, and the result was edgy singing drowned by an accompaniment lacking all subtlety of tone colour. The bassoonist had seen this too often to be despondent about it; he knew that, with increasing familiarity, the music would improve out of all recognition.

On arriving for the dress rehearsal, he made his way to the pit which he knew so well and where he had spent so many happy hours. He was dismayed to find it altered. Because of emergency building works in the theatre, a temporary low staging of scaffolding and planks had been erected in the pit. As he picked his way to his seat to the right of the MD, he heard a commotion at the opposite end of the pit: the double bass player was complaining about a gap between the planks exactly where he wanted to place the end-pin of his instrument.

The bassoonist guessed what would happen next and, sure enough, the cellist was soon airing the same complaint. And after he himself sat down and unpacked and assembled his bassoon, he found that he too had the same problem with his floor-spike. Only by contorting himself to an uncomfortable angle was he able to limp through the dress rehearsal.

He pondered his options for holding his bassoon for the rest of the week: he had never been comfortable with a seat strap, and he found a knee rest even worse. Nothing for it; when he got home, he would have to swap his floor-spike for a neck strap.

He approached this practical task with superstitious dread. It awoke memories that he had wanted to forget, that went to the heart of his lonely existence.

He had started the bassoon in secondary school, in a class of two. His classmate was a girl so pretty that he was soon besotted. In playing the bassoon, they were taught to use neck straps rather than floor-spikes and, as an impressionable adolescent, he was uncomfortably aware how the neck strap showed her figure off to advantage. Politely yet firmly, she deflected all his many approaches. When their paths diverged as they went to different universities, his way of putting her out of his mind was to reject the neck strap and adopt the floor-spike.

Put simply, he had been suffering from a teenage crush, but in his case he had never grown out of it.

The next evening, the first public performance, he joined 'his' group. This orchestra was unusual in that the strings and the wind did not automatically form separate cliques; here, ever since they discovered that they were all science graduates from the same university, 'his' group had consisted of all the players of the bass clef. They vigorously engaged in a favourite activity of all musicians, they grumbled about their playing conditions.

As performance time approached, they went to their respective places and prepared their instruments. He was surprised to recall how different his bassoon felt with a neck strap, with his right hand having to press down much harder to keep the bassoon at a suitable angle. With this change to his routine, and the subtly different position of the reed in his lips, he felt quite unsettled. This showed up in his playing, which was bespattered with elementary mistakes, hardly up to an adequate standard even allowing for it being so early in the week. He went home that night ashamed of his poor performance and unable to get to sleep as he relived each error in his mind.

As the week progressed, just as he had foreseen, the performance quality (including his own) did indeed improve by leaps and bounds. The orchestra were mostly long-standing friends. The theatre was comfortable and pleasantly warm, apart from the inconvenient staging on which they had to perch in the pit – and, with familiarity, even that was becoming less of a nuisance. The MD was calm and clear. The production was well-directed with good pace. The actors were speaking and singing confidently and well.

Yet something was wrong – the usual magic wasn't happening, the feeling of total escape and fulfilment that he only ever found in one place in his life: in the orchestra pit once a successful production was in its stride.

What could it be? The building works in the theatre? The one new player? This was the oboist, right in front of him. He had noticed her buying a programme to check the names of the orchestra, which struck him as odd since he had gathered that she was a last-minute recruit, too late for her own name to be included. She irritated him by leaning back in her chair during long dialogues, forcing him to adjust the angle of the light on his music stand to avoid the distraction of her hair suddenly looming into view, brilliantly illuminated, above his band part.

But no, he couldn't blame the oboist for his sense of malaise. She was a fine workmanlike player, appeared almost pathetically glad to be there, and paid extraordinary attention all the time to her reed, not that that was a fault.

On Saturday, all the familiar 'last-night' cues were there: the scent of expensive perfume wafting from the front stalls into the pit, the shuffling and scraping as the mayor's entourage took their seats, the generally heightened sense of occasion. But even these failed to evoke the expected feeling of wellbeing in him.

The overture started. He played mechanically, joylessly. Soon Professor Higgins would utter his words "... crooning like a bilious pigeon," the cue for Eliza to cry out and for the bassoon to execute a short but totally unaccompanied upward semiquaver passage in D major. His reed was on form, he played the passage acceptably, but still something was missing. Even his downward semiquaver solos in F major, later in the same number, though technically correct, didn't satisfy him.

At last, one of his favourite moments. Perhaps this would be it. Eliza Doolittle threw her book on the floor, the cue for Number 7, her song 'Just You Wait, 'Enry 'Iggins', in Db, the usual key for important songs in shows. This song was every other bassoonist's nightmare, not only because of the key, and not only because D♮ itself was the most uncertain note on the bassoon, but because of its Alberti bass accompaniment. Not just any ordinary arpeggiated Alberti bass, but with notorious leaps of two octaves.

He always looked forward to this song, ever since he had discovered that, in most editions, the nightmare passage was cued into the other band parts, letting him demonstrate to all the musicians what he was capable of.

He proudly tossed off a tricky chromatic phrase occurring earlier in the song. In a few bars, the nightmare passage. Breathe in. Tongue ready. His moment of glory. Count off the preceding two-four bar. Pull on the handpiece to ease the bassoon into a more comfortable position. Watch for the downbeat. Go!

Out poured his accomplished semiquavers – he began to feel better – until he felt a sudden jarring under his right hand. Before he could collect his thoughts, he felt his handpiece wobble and spin off his bassoon, crashing noisily to the floor. His semiquavers degenerated into a hideous series of squawks interspersed with the sound of clashing levers and spinning rollers, as he struggled to hold his bassoon steady. Somehow he limped through the rest of the song, not however even attempting the recapitulation of his showpiece passage.

After that song, he leaned down to pick up his handpiece. Misjudging, he nudged it sideways. It rolled away, to fall through a gap between the planks of the temporary staging, out of reach.

By adopting an uncomfortable grip, he was able to exert enough control over his bassoon in the remaining numbers of the first Act to play those notes that mattered most; this being the last evening, he had, by now, come to know exactly which they were. His whole brittle world was falling apart; his single form of self-identity – reliable master-craftsman bassoonist – was being destroyed by this evening's events.

At the end of the First Act Finale, he saw the oboist lean round to him, but he had no time for social niceties right now; as the house lights came up for the interval, he rushed out of the pit to implement an idea he had worked out for a possible running repair.

The oboist, seeing the dreadful expression on his face, feared he was going out to do something rash. She picked up her bag and followed at a discreet distance as he stormed out of the stage door into the car park.

She stopped just outside the stage door, where it was dark. She relaxed, leaning against the outside wall of the theatre. She sipped some coffee from her flask; the steam rose lazily in the cool evening air. A few yards away, Colonel Pickering and two girls from the chorus, in their costumes, were enjoying a surreptitious cigarette.

When she saw the bonnet of the bassoonist's car being raised and a torch coming on, she became concerned and hurried over. The bassoonist saw, looming suddenly up and lit by his torch, exactly the same picture of shining hair that he had earlier seen lit by his music stand, so knew exactly who had come out to visit him.

"Have you come out to laugh, to revel in my ruin?" he shouted.

"No, of course not, but what are you doing?"

"I'm looking for anything that might do as a makeshift handpiece," he explained. "Here, this T-piece coupling, see, just behind the air filter, this looks good, I'll wrench it off and bring it in."

"Look, you'll get filthy. And you'll probably wreck your car. And you haven't time – the interval must be half over by now."

"So what do you suggest, clever-clogs?"

"I'll fix you up. I will. Just come back in. Do you know," she added, after he had calmed down, closed the bonnet and locked his car, "I'd never dared talk to you before. Always, erm,

I mean all week, you were so infallible and self-assured, and now you're human after all."

"I'd rather be infallible and self-assured," he said with bad grace.

Back in the pit, she took from her toolbag a length of straightened-out coat-hanger-wire which she kept for if her pull-through should jam. She fashioned the wire into a grip and wedged it into its locating hole on the bassoon using a corner of her handkerchief.

"How come you're such an expert on bassoons?" he asked.

"Just let me finish this. Make yourself useful, warm my reed," she ordered, presenting it into his lips.

Shocked by the intimacy and forced into silence, he watched as she tied the remainder of her handkerchief around the improvised wire grip to make it more comfortable.

As he played the second half, he could taste her in his mouth from her reed, and he could smell her as his hand warmed the scent in her handkerchief. And he continued to see her hair framing his band part. He was able to play well, but he was doing so on auto-pilot; his mind was in turmoil.

At the end of the show, he found he could recall nothing of the applause, the end-of-show speeches, or whether they had played the regular Exit Music or the National Anthem. These were details which, for all his previous shows, he had meticulously filed in his memory.

Immediately the audience had left, a stagehand gathered up the band parts, and another unplugged the music stands and carried them away. The stage curtains were opened and the house lights turned up full. Cold outside air, from the scenery loading dock being opened, chilled the cosy pit. In these few moments, all the illusion of the week's show was rudely stripped away.

The other woodwind players packed quickly and hurried off. The oboist turned her chair towards the bassoonist as they went through their maintenance and packing routines. The artificial barrier of his music stand between them was gone. Looking at her, he saw someone just a few years younger than himself, handsome rather than conventionally pretty, with character and yet – as his eye stole furtively to her left hand – no ring.

He could not face ending this week in the pit like all his other weeks in pits, with everybody dispersing home and him feeling in a few minutes more miserable than if the whole week had never happened. He desperately wanted to say something to her but didn't know what or how. But it was she who spoke first:

"You've still got my handkerchief."

"Oh, yes. You really saved me, I mean, you really did, thanks," he blurted out. "Will you, would you, er, that is, let's go and have a drink together."

"Yes, I'd like that," she replied, "but do you still really not know who I am?"

The Trombonist

She really is something. She must be singing Nancy. What have I been doing, we're about to start the second half of the band call and I've not noticed her before.

"Oi, reporter man!" I shout. "You can change what I said, put 'women' at the top of my list!"

He doesn't hear me. He's just interviewed me, he explains that this operatic society is always big news in the town, especially its first production in this new theatre. What's my instrument, he asks. 'Marine Parade,' I'm tempted to reply. And what are my concerns? I list them for him: "Beer. Motorbikes. Women. Oh yes, dentists. And of course beer."

I can afford to be flippant, this week's *Oliver* should be a rest cure, at least compared with the *West Side Story* I did last week. It was the usual brass stuff, sit around silent for half an hour and then have to hit the button spot-on first time at the dramatic entries, no second chances to get it right. You have to be bold and cool and enjoy it, no room for irresolutes or self-doubters in the brass, thank you.

Already in the first half of this *Oliver*, I've had to do plenty of trombone-speciality sound effects. No.2 'Food Glorious Food' needs me to open my plunger for that flatulent-type noise immediately after they sing the word "indigestion". You can get trombone plungers from specialist dealers, but I always use an ordinary kitchen plunger, just as good and much cheaper. Oh yes, the growl in no.3 'Oliver,' I have to roll my tongue in a special way. Then more plunger stuff, closing and opening the bell for the "wow" noise in no.11 'You've Got to Pick a Pocket or Two,' just moments before I need the cup mute.

Ah, back to work now. The MD lifts her baton for the first number of the second Act, Nancy's 'Oom-Pah-Pah.' I like the superbly vulgar trombone glissandi in this number, pity they're hardly the stuff to impress Nancy.

Monday evening

Talk about modern architecture, I can't find the stage door. I go into the foyer where we did yesterday's band call and ask someone. They show me a security door in a corner of the foyer. And that really is the stage door. I knock, they let me in, tell me the door code and give me directions. I follow a maze of corridors and staircases. Odd, it's taking me through the children's dressing room; ah, it's right enough, the door on the far side takes me into the pit.

I find the music stand with the trombone part on it. I'm under the stage overhang, I'm not going to see Nancy at all, all week. I'm facing the audience in theory, but they won't see me either, it's too deep. The leader (the one and only violin) is directly in front of me, the cellist and bass to one side at right angles, and the keyboard next to me. It's all so unusual that nobody dares question the MD about it.

Except she's not there yet. She rushes in late, apologises, says the producer needed to have a conference with her. Turns out it's her first ever sight of the pit. She's too shocked by her vertiginous podium and tall rickety stool to worry about the pit layout. She assumes that was the musicians' own preference. We learn later that the pit was laid out and the parts put on the stands randomly by the theatre staff, who had never had to do it before.

I begin to notice some awkward bits in this trombone

part. Don't think much of those chromatics in no.2 at the last key change into F. Then something new, we never played it at the band call because no singers were involved, some ugly semiquavers in D♭ in no.8A 'Fight.' The MD takes those at that awkward in-between speed that's too fast for ordinary tonguing and not fast enough for double-tonguing.

We come eventually to no.27 'London Bridge,' another non-vocal number we skipped at the band call to save time. It's set in Victorian London at midnight. Stage smoke, what a cliché, comes floating into the pit, and it's all I can do to sight-read through it – triplets in minor thirds, all in different positions.

My lips are in fine condition for the high B♭ in no.30 'Consider Yourself reprise.' They're tight, I'm in control. As long as they last the week. And they might, the MD is letting us off the Exit Music tonight, because it's so late.

Shame, also because it's so late, nobody in the band will join me for a drink. Ah well, later in the week perhaps.

Tuesday evening

Opening night. The piped music is turned up loud on the auditorium PA. It's impossible for us to tune. Eventually, I calibrate the auditorium music to my electronic tuner and tune my trombone to the piped music.

Punctually, the green light comes up on the MD's stand to start the Overture. The bassoonist hasn't arrived yet. The MD whispers, "Look, we'll just have to start."

I wonder whether I'll have to play the bassoon's pomposo passages, illustrating Mr Bumble's walk, in no.2 'Food Glorious Food.' The trouble will be to swap parts back, find my right place in time and play my own chromaticky solo immediately afterwards.

The bassoonist does arrive, breathless, and assembles his instrument in the nick of time. What breath control, he conquers his panting through his solo, but there's an unmistakeable buzz. He looks gloomily at his acres of rods, levers and linkages, it could be any one of them.

I decide to oil my slide, but I apply only the thick oil by the time the smoke in 'London Bridge' distracts me. The rapid minor-third triplets in that number are like a weight-lifting exercise, my slide is so stiff. I nearly swear. I've never before failed to apply the thin oil at the bottom of the slide as well as the thick at the top. The two are supposed to mix to give optimum lubrication. Not for the first time, I wonder why the thick oil, of which you need less, comes in large bottles, while the thin oil, of which you need more, comes in small ones.

After the final curtain comes the first time in any show that I have ever played the publisher's provided Exit Music; usually MDs substitute their own. The publisher's Exit Music is a good choice, I can tell, it's received with loud cheers and applause, which means that some of the out-of-sight audience have stayed around in the auditorium to hear it through. A moment later, a gaggle of Brownies appears looking over the pit rail, gazing at us with interest and admiration. The keyboard player whispers that these are surely my groupies.

What a show, all I have is a couple of glisses in 'Oom-Pah-Pah' and a high note in the 'Consider Yourself' reprise. Did I learn the trombone to make such a tiny impact? No, I play to be *heard*, preferably seen as well, and not by just a few Brownies.

Even now, nobody will join me for a drink. Are they all tee-totallers, or spoilsports, or what? I can just see it, no real Big Moments to show off in this music, and no social side. I shall go home at the end of this week with nothing to remember it by.

Wednesday evening

Now I'm used to the music and the pace of the show, I can start to pay more attention to what's going on. In the early number 'I Shall Scream,' the pickups have so far been frankly ragged, and having a one-crotchet rest I've been unable to help. Tonight the double bass ignores the MD and times his first note by instinct. Everyone follows him, and I can now easily place my own second and third beats correctly.

Children start to drift into the pit from the changing room to watch the band at work, and the keyboard player, in her distinctive whisper, says to me, "Ah, more of your groupies."

She's vaguely familiar in a girl-next-door sort of way. Someone says she was the society's rehearsal accompanist. Sure enough, she tells me who auditioned unsuccessfully, who had to be recast, and who had blazing rows with whom. I even get day-by-day minute-by-minute whispered commentaries about whether a principal is feeling off-colour and may need extra-sympathetic accompaniment. She might tell me all about Nancy, if only I ask her in the right way.

Now a group of young women in costume drifts into the pit. Pity, Nancy isn't among them. Another pity, they're not there to admire me but to invisibly beef up the children's choir on stage.

The high point of the evening turns out to be Fagin's song 'Reviewing the Situation.' After the first violin cadenza, Fagin ad-libs, "What's this, *Fiddler on the Roof?*" upon which, quick as thought, the violinist vamps 'If I were a Rich Man.' Not to be outdone, Fagin launches into his next verse with absolutely no warning, throwing us completely. The audience roars with laughter. I had rests at these places so couldn't help, but then the double bass takes over at the start of Fagin's next verses with such command that we all follow, and Fagin is left high-and-dry. The violinist makes the most of her next two cadenzas and, a rare honour from hard-boiled pit musicians, we shuffle our feet.

In the London Bridge scene shortly afterwards, the smoke is so thick it pours like a waterfall off the stage into the pit. The MD had always cued me in after a 5-bar rest in this number – very necessary, it was never exactly 5 bars, I guess it had to fit some action on-stage. In the smoke, I completely lose sight of the MD and can hardly even see the notes in front of me. At the end, as we're all packing our instruments, the MD says she'll have electric fans brought into the pit to dispel the smoke.

Half way through the week, I've still not exchanged a word with Nancy; she's too inaccessible. But right in front of me, the violinist is putting on her coat. I don't risk asking her to the pub, but I exchange a few tentative words with her. She's quite affably responsive.

Thursday evening

The good news is my dental check-up was OK. Dental work can upset a brass player's embouchure, can even finish his career. The bad news is that the dentist's prodding and probing rubbed my lip, and my fast motorbike ride to the theatre made it worse. Old-timers in the brass world would always say you shouldn't even kiss if you wanted to keep your lip in tip-top condition. Fat chance, the way things are going for me this week.

To think, I gave up playing rugger to avoid injuring my lips or teeth and here I am, with unserviceable lips anyway. Sport and music are so alike: whether it's to score a try or play music, you have to apply physical effort with dexterity, accuracy and discipline, in real-time, no chance to go back and put right any mistakes.

The fans brought in for the smoke are so effective that

the pages of all the parts flap around in the draught. OK for me, I'm used to outdoor gigs, I just reach into my tackle bag for clothes-pegs, but it all makes for slower and more awkward page-turning.

I'd always noticed how the cellist looks like the violinist, but had put it down to all string players looking the same. Now I'm totally confused, until the keyboard girl whispers that the violinist and cellist have swapped tonight for fun. That explains why the violin solo in Oliver's tear-jerker 'Where Is Love' sounded different, with a harder steady tone.

Meanwhile, the regular violinist, playing cello tonight, is making quite a showpiece of the 'Consider Yourself At Home' number, and I'm put off by her effortless versatility. On the spot, I decide to try my luck with the regular cellist, now sitting in front of me playing violin.

She's a complete charmer. What have I been doing, wasting all week?

Come the second Act, her Fagin cadenzas have a no-nonsense commanding competence that makes me wonder what's behind the charm. I wonder, can it be, the violinist and cellist, are they sisters, are they perhaps even twins? This is getting too deep for me.

After all the trouble with the fans, there's no smoke in the 'London Bridge' number tonight.

My lips have started to bleed and finally give out in the reprise, near the very end, of 'Consider Yourself ...' I very publicly split my showpiece high notes. Well, that certainly finally blows my chances with the violin and cello girls.

Friday evening
After a day of applying lip salve, I'm back on form. I'm relieved to see the fans have been unplugged.

The percussionist has brought in a portable electronic special-effects machine for its horses'-hooves-and-carriages sound. From then on, he uses it in every, but every, street scene.

During the interval, the MD announces to us that ticket sales have been so good that a Saturday matinée performance is being added. At this very late stage, I'm one of the few still free; many of the band are down to play in the Mayor's Gala Charity Orchestra that same afternoon. Even one of the principal singers is billed to sing at the Gala. The keyboard player isn't in the Mayor's Orchestra, so she's one of the few others still free.

After the interval, the celebrated "…the law is an ass…" speech is delivered correctly for the first time in the week. The percussionist cheekily gives a celebratory side-drum roll and cymbals crash. He doesn't care that he'll never be used by that MD again, he's just landed a job on a cruise liner.

In the 'London Bridge' sequence, with the fans out of action, we get smoke …

Saturday afternoon

A line of deps straggles into the pit. They witness the unusual sight of a dep principal singer being rehearsed through some of her entries by the MD.

My eye roves towards the dep double bass. She's competent as well as pretty. But, in the middle of some dialogue, her mobile phone goes off, clattering off her music stand onto the hard floor. There's another cymbals crash. No-one takes her seriously after that. Maybe I can. Ouch, bad move.

In front of me is the dep violin, looking like an ice queen, glacially unapproachable. Her playing matches her appearance. I tell her so. She turns back to glare at me. I tell her to open out, not live in an ice-shell. She ignores me. She plays all her little touches with a cold restraint, even her solo in Oliver's cloyingly sentimental song 'Where Is Love?' I admire the stage poise of the boy, or maybe girl, playing Oliver, who's now coped with three quite different styles of violin accompaniment in his/her Big Ballad.

After that song, the children always return to the changing room adjoining the pit. They've never been totally quiet, but this afternoon their boisterousness is surely audible in the auditorium. I get up and peep through the door, just in time to see the actor who must be Bill Sykes arriving through the other door. Heard from the pit, he has always sounded out-and-out evil, and seen in the flesh he's absolutely terrifying. The children fall instantly silent. What a contrast with the usual sort of embarrassed Bill Sykes actor, who's all too obviously really a genial shopkeeper or a decent sort in the middle reaches of the Town Hall.

As I return to my seat, I hear a rainstorm and distant thunder. At the interval, I tentatively look out of one of the backstage emergency exits. It's sunny and fine. Hm, the percussionist's mischievous electronic effects. I find the keyboard player already sitting outside taking the air.

"I was fooled by the thunder too. But look, June is bustin' out all over," she jokes.

"Eventful show, that," I reply.

"Oh? Tell me."

"Oh," I start to reminisce, "I did *Carousel* last year, but it was in the old theatre, this one still wasn't ready. I think it might even have been for this operatic society, I'm not sure. Anyway, it was opening night. I had this 98 bar rest in Billy Biggelow's Soliloquy, and my counting just went. I got more and more lost. The kids I teach, they're lost all the time and they must be used to the feeling, but my counting's so good I'd never been lost for years. I'd forgotten what it's like. There's tricks for counting your way back in, but I was years out of practice. Utterly and completely lost I was, with a vital entry coming up. There's my heart beating nineteen to the dozen, sweat pouring off me..." I tail off, ashamed.

"Oh, please carry on, it's fascinating!"

"Well, anyway," I continue, desperate to shift the subject away from my own failings, "come the second Act, the double bass has this solo, well actually he has two, in Louise's big ballet scene. I have this 24 bar rest meanwhile, that's how I was able to notice. He *looks* impassive of course, they all do 'cos they know they're on view all the time, but I can tell he's lost too now, and petrified with it. Nothing I can do to help, of course, nothing cued in or anything. He muffs his solos, big-time. Don't know how the dancer coped, but she did and we got the end in one piece."

She smiles – why? She makes me continue.

"Well, that was just the start really. We all went out together for a curry on the Friday night. Four of us get ill, yes, one was the leader and one was the MD. Of course nobody realises how serious this is till the whole picture comes together, about half an hour before the Saturday matinée. Sheer fluke, someone found out that the society's own rehearsal accompanist just happened to be in the house, no it wasn't you, I'd remember you, it was a man that time, so he has to come forward and conduct what's left of the band, violins all moving up a seat and having to sight-read, second trumpet having to cover first, the lot. Then there's the scene where Jigger blows cigarette smoke all over Mrs Mullin and, this time, it blows all into the pit. No, not like this smoke here, but it made everybody cough like mad. Poor old oboist has to plunge straight into the Soliloquy, poignant stuff on the cor anglais, straight in. Wonderful song, well it's more than just a song, but anyway, so many tempo changes ahead, 98 bars – oh, I already said – and so many awkward corners and traps, I think, if we get through this, short-staffed and with a temporary MD, I vow I'll never swear again. Next Act, I'm waiting for Louise's ballet to go wrong again, except by this time I've heard it often enough to vamp the bass solo if..."

"Five minutes," says the backstage PA, at which she skips with a graceful lightness back to the pit.

I finish my can of drink and follow. If the percussionist can have a bit of fun, so can I. I pretend to tune to the keyboard A, but imperceptibly wobble my slide so as to induce the rest of the band to tune to my false A. But Miss Ice Queen Violin, sitting directly in front of me, she notices.

First number, Nancy's 'Oom-Pah-Pah.' Push slide out for my showpiece gliss. I pull back but find I'm stuck on the bottom note. Why has my slide jammed? I'd oiled it OK. I heave desperately. Then I see that Miss Ice Queen has hooked her shoe round the bottom end of my slide. Sabotage in the original true meaning of the word. She's ruined my number and finally ruined any chance I might have had with Nancy.

I'm caught unprepared for the Fagin cadenzas. Miss Ice Queen plays with a sweep and breadth and feeling, and with such tonal accuracy, that I can hardly believe the tale I heard, that the leader in the inaugural production of *Oliver* had improvised them out of boredom while Fagin ruminated on-stage, and that the composer then added them to the score. Despite what she did to me, I shuffle my feet in genuine appreciation.

She swivels round and hisses, "I don't care for that. Or for you. Keep your mind on the job."

I seethe silently. I console myself that I'm pro rata better than she is. String players, apart from being prigs, are stupid, because they think that the quality wind playing they always hear means that wind playing is easy. The real reason is that there's such a surplus of wind players that only the best get anywhere near symphony orchestras or groups with strings. I never admit in public that this doesn't quite apply to trombones, who are currently in short supply; it's too complicated to explain to brainless string players that the trombone, being considered less glamorous in the brass fraternity, is suitable only for the most gifted and motivated players.

I stop seething when we reach the 'As Long as He Needs Me reprise,' in which Nancy transfers her loyalty from the hardened desperado Bill Sykes, who hardly needs it, to the boy Oliver, who so vulnerably does. I noticed how Nancy was always rushed by the MD in this reprise, when it could have benefitted from a little freedom.

The dep double bass shows she has unexpected steel in her character. She ignores the MD's haste and adds her own delays, carefully following all Nancy's breaths and pauses and nuances. We ignore the MD's flailings and follow the bass. The massive applause afterwards says it all.

Saturday evening

For the last night's 'London Bridge' sequence, they use up all their remaining stocks of smoke. Opaque clouds of it fill the pit. The MD vanishes into the fog. For a while I can see the shadow of her arm against her music stand light, but even this fades into invisibility. The music continues with reasonable accuracy since, by now, we know exactly how the music fits into the dialogue and with the various bumps and groans from the stage above our heads. It's the scene where Bill Sykes murders Nancy but can't prevent Oliver's reunion with his grandfather.

The smoke continues to thicken until we can't even read our own music. The fans can't cope and simply ensure that we all enjoy identical density of smoke. The effect of this on the music is to heighten the sense of uncertainty and horror. The MD loves it, warns us that if she ever conducts *Oliver* again, she'll have similar white-out quantities of smoke.

At the end of the show, we hear the applause die down suddenly, and before we can launch into the Exit Music, we hear new deliberate footsteps above their heads. This means one thing: some serious on-stage end-of-run speechifying. The MD whispers that we must still play the playout at the end, so we can't pack our instruments and creep out. While the speeches drone on, we agree at last to visit the pub afterwards. Only one musician declines, having a band call on the Sunday morning.

Someone hands down a magnificent bouquet of flowers to the MD. She balances on her stool and waves – the audience might just see her arm above the pit rail. For all her foibles, we've enjoyed working for her and we join the applause.

In good humour, we go down to the pub. The bar rings with tall stories, chat and gossip. I make up for my week's abstinence and hardly notice the musicians peeling off home one by one, until only one of my colleagues is left. Through my agreeable alcoholic haze, I still know that I'm in no fit state to ride my motorbike home, and I allow myself to be helped into the passenger seat of a car.

After that, I remember nothing, until I become dreamily aware of the close proximity of a girl. Not just any girl, but the one who had danced the part of Louise in last year's *Carousel*. But that's impossible – I'd never even spoken to her. I turn away from her to see where I am. I recognise nothing, except my trombone case neatly stacked in a corner. My lip feels even harder-used than at the end of the show.

While my half-asleep brain struggles to make sense of it all, I hear her whisper to me. Now I know! Louise is one and the same as the keyboard player.

The Leader

As she arrived for the band call, she could summon up none of her usual enthusiasm. It was yet another *Mikado*. She knew the dialogue as well as any prompt, having played it more frequently than any other show, although *Oliver* was coming a close second. She was in great demand to lead pit orchestras for her experience and steady decisive tone.

She recognised the double bass, the bassoon and the trombone as experienced grizzlies, but was surprised to know so few of the other musicians. Even more surprising, nobody who might be a singer seemed to have arrived.

"OK, hello everybody," said the MD, "welcome. Glad you all found this place all right, unusual to have a theatre like this stuck on top of a block of offices. Anyway, I know, for a lot of you, it's your first show. I want to spread the experience of this sort of orchestral playing. This show, well it really plays itself, so it'll be a good introduction for you. We'll have a quick play-through until the coffee break, when the singers will join us. Overture please, in four, two upbeats for nothing."

The Leader had never known a band call where the music broke down as early as Bar 2. Until that moment, she would have agreed with the MD that *The Mikado* played itself, but she now came to realise this was only because any novices would be swept along by the majority of the orchestra, who had played it many times already.

Within a few moments, it had broken down again, when the viola had a solo rhythmic passage in an unexpectedly different tempo. The leader whispered something to the other first violin, who had to admit that he had played *The Mikado* only once before, and then as second violin.

The opening chorus took her by surprise, for its empty orchestral sound. She had never heard it without singers before. As the rehearsal limped on, singers began to arrive, and the orchestra-only run-through was guillotined for lack of time at the end of Act One.

The Leader preferred to forget the rest of the day, although there were lighter moments: In the Act Two song which describes the execution which actually never happened, the flautist, piccolist and oboist have awkward grotesque solo passages which are almost impossible to fit in. The players, pretty young girls, each in turn yelped in alarm when they reached their respective solos, which they had not reached during the orchestra-only run-through. They had to be reassured that it was only the effect that mattered, not note-perfection. The MD seemed to enjoy administering this reassurance.

Next day, the Leader arrived with some apprehension at the first dress rehearsal. (This company had the tradition of two dress rehearsals, the first being run without the lengthier dialogues.) The overture had no life or sparkle, but at least all the tunes were there and it got to the end in one piece. Actors tried to take position on stage for the opening chorus while the Stage Manager and choreographer, oblivious, were blocking the wing entrance holding an animated discussion.

One actor asked the producer if, in this first dress rehearsal, he should also do the accompanying moves and other stage business.

The producer, a lady with the composed and uncontradictable air of a hospital matron, boomed, "Oh yes, I want all the business I can get."

There was a moment's shocked silence, then helpless laughter. This broke the tension, and the rehearsal proceeded with good humour, despite even the many attempts needed of the duet between Nanki-Poo and Yum-Yum, with its awkward tempo changes.

As the second dress rehearsal unfolded on stage, the Leader's admiration for the producer grew. The Leader had seen every possible treatment of the play, but this production, while hardly deviating from the correct words, had all sorts of novel touches.

Thus, when Ko-Ko was brought a letter from the Mikado, he did not simply rip it open, he bowed reverentially while holding it. Quite right too, so he would. And when Yum-Yum was summoned to be asked, "Are you particularly busy?" she responded quietly and downcast. Well, quite right, her lover was sentenced to death, of course she would be downcast, unlike the usual productions where she would answer brightly. Then, in the (false) certificate of Nanki-Poo's execution, one of the witnesses was not the "groom of the second floor front," an allusion lost on a twenty-first-century audience, but "webmaster@titipu.com."

When the Mikado ordered those witnesses to "Describe it!", the Leader by reflex action started to play the song. She missed the MD waiting while the witnesses gestured frantically to each other. Quite right, the witnesses were having to make it all up on the spot, and could not immediately launch into a descriptive song. When the witnesses, thinking they had been reprieved, heard the Mikado tell them, "I forget the punishment...," they fell prostrate in ragged confusion. Quite right, they would not have kneeled in a tidy choreographed movement. Finally, in the last few sequences, the Mikado made obvious his irritation at Katisha's overbearing egomania. Quite right, he would never have tolerated such disrespect for his own position.

The second evening of the show, on getting up to conduct the first number after the entr'acte, the MD stumbled and kicked over the clarinettist's full beer glass. There was chaos on the wind side, covered by extra loud playing by the strings until the wind players filtered in one by one. The leader exchanged superior looks with her fellow first-violinist. Despite mopping-up efforts, the pit smelt like a pub for the rest of that evening, and the players' shoes stuck to the floor whenever they had to walk past that spot.

The next evening, the Leader dropped her rosin, which shattered into powder as it hit the floor. This not only stuck the players' shoes as viciously as did the beer but also crunched noisily when walked upon. The wind players did not comment in words, but through nuances in their playing.

The performances followed the usual path of increasing slickness on stage and increasing accuracy from the orchestra, although the orchestral starting level for a familiar show such as *The Mikado* was normally much higher. It always surprised the Leader how audiences laughed at the jokes as if for the first time, when she had heard them a hundred times before.

Her fellow first violinist was proving a competent if unimaginative player. His page-turning for her was impeccable. He would be worth cultivating, especially when he had acquired that steely toughness that characterises habitual first violinists. She supposed it came from having to play almost all the tunes throughout, with every note having to be spot-on correct, or maybe it came from the mental effort of just having to play more notes than any of the other instrumentalists.

The two first-violinists exchanged business cards and, over the days, life histories. She learned that his wife had been promoted to a stressful responsible job. This had worsened the tension about the many evenings he was out playing his violin, to the point where he was beginning to wonder how much longer she would put up with it. If anything could keep them together, he confided, it was that they both doted on their small children. The Leader's two teenagers, oh how different, she was always having to worry about them, the boy was forever getting up to mischief, and the girl had been oddly quiet and out of sorts lately.

One evening, the theatre air-conditioning had broken down and it was hot even before the start. One of the musicians tentatively pushed at an emergency exit door in the lobby leading to the pit, in the hope of getting some fresh air. This door opened onto a paved area which turned out to be a rooftop balcony with a surrealistic view, including a disused railway line far below, a modern entertainment centre opposite (complete with cinemas and burger bars), and offices across the way being busily hoovered by the night cleaners. There was also a grandstand view of a multi-storey car-park, factories and, as an incongruous backdrop to all these, a pleasant wooded hillside. This balcony henceforth became the orchestral common room area.

As that night's performance proceeded in the stifling auditorium, the rosin on the Leader's strings, softened by the heat, had become so sticky it was tearing hairs out of her bow. The other first violinist offered her meths, expecting her to wipe her strings with it. Pretending to misunderstand, she said, "No thanks, I've given it up for Lent," before showing her superior upbringing by using eau-de-cologne for the purpose.

The heat was taking its toll of the instrumental tuning, and the humidity was taking its toll of orchestral tempers. At the interval, the double bass came up to the Leader and threatened to walk out because of the bassoon's poor intonation. The other first violinist, hitherto unaware of this side of a Leader's duties, watched her deploy a skilful mixture of flattery, cajolery and humour to win the double bass round. If only *he* could communicate half as well with his wife.

On the Saturday afternoon, there was a long queue for the multi-storey car-park, with cars being admitted only one by one as others departed. When it was at last her turn and the barrier opened for her, the Leader congratulated herself on seeing a space almost at once, next to a wall. As she reversed into it, she saw why it had stayed vacant. Her neighbour was a 4x4 so badly parked that she could open her door just a few inches. While wriggling out, she snagged her long black skirt on her door lock mechanism. She then had great difficulties in reaching back in to retrieve her violin and bag.

Because the fronts of her car and of the 4x4 were nearly touching, she had to sidle to the back, to get out via the far side of the 4x4. As the 4x4 was backed close up to the rear wall, she had to squeeze under its protruding rear-mounted spare wheel while hitching her long skirt to step over its tow bar. At last, with violin and bag, she emerged at the far side of the 4x4 and was able to walk normally out of the car park to the theatre.

After all this, she only half-listened when the other first violinist recounted his tale of woe, how things were not going well at home and his wife was having to attend a Saturday professional conference, leaving him to do the weekly wash but the machine had flooded and when he discovered this, he only had time, between feeding his children their lunch and having to take his children to the childminder's on his way to the theatre, to phone one repair company and their first appointment wasn't until next Wednesday.

Why was he going on so? Her own children were much more of a worry – she was beginning to think her daughter might be pregnant.

While her brain was in "worry" mode, the thought crept into her mind that, what with all her difficulties and distractions in the car park, she'd forgotten to lock her car. This thought grew and nagged away at her. She would have to check as soon as possible. The magnificent Finale of the First Act left her cold – she was waiting for the interval when she could dash out. She knew she had a reputation as a worrier, and therefore didn't tell anyone where she was going or why. She put her violin in her case, leaving it open so as not to waste a moment, picked out her car keys from her handbag and made her way swiftly to the foyer and there summoned a lift. It came at once and took her down to the ground floor non-stop. Great!

A momentary delay at the automated exit door and she was out in the chilling air of a late Saturday afternoon. She was able to cross the road almost straight away to the multi-storey. As soon as she came up to the right level, she could see her car. This meant that the badly parked 4x4 had gone, thank goodness. Breathless from her haste, she tried her car door.

It had been locked all the time. Relief flooding through her, she returned to the theatre.

The automated entry door wouldn't let her in.

She had never expected this problem. A noticeboard by the door listed the opening hours of the council offices which occupied all of the building except for the top-floor theatre. Sure enough, the offices were shut on Saturday afternoon. She couldn't phone the theatre, as she'd come out without her phone or money for a callbox. She hoped she might see a policeman. She was wondering in her mind how to explain her predicament to him, but soon realised she wouldn't find one in time. She considered throwing something against the windows to attract attention, but they were far too high. She then wondered wildly about going into the entertainment centre across the road and trying to find a window facing the musicians' rooftop balcony. Did the entertainment centre have any such windows anyway? She couldn't remember.

At length, she resigned herself to abject defeat. She went to her car and sat in it. She couldn't drive anywhere, as she had no money for the barrier. She listened to the car radio for what would be the duration of the Second Act of *The Mikado*. She heard Glazunov's Saxophone Concerto. She had never known that such a piece existed.

Meanwhile, inside the theatre, the end-of-interval warning

bell rang. The oboe blew a tuning A. The other first violinist vaguely wondered about not having seen the Leader. When not recounting her worries to him, she was normally in the centre of the "balcony clique," swapping stories about their children's exploits. She was obviously around – her violin case was open and her bag was looped round her chair. Perhaps there had been a long queue for the Ladies? Perhaps she was in the bar, this being the last night of the show? Perhaps she had been taken ill? Yes, that was possible, she had played one, it might even have been two, wrong notes in the First Act, quite unlike her normal self.

He decided to ask the viola whether the Leader had mentioned anything about feeling unwell. As he stepped past the second-violin desk, he caught his foot in its taut electric cable. This brought several music stands down like ninepins. All the band parts fell off the stands and some sheets of paper fluttered to the ground. These were the musicians' carefully compiled reminder notes and photocopies to save impossible page-turns.

One of the music stands landed heavily on the Leader's violin case. There was a shocked silence in the pit, and sensing something amiss, the audience too hushed. With a sense of dread, he gingerly re-righted the stand and inspected the Leader's violin. The bridge was still standing but the fingerboard was loose. By itself, not a problem – it could be easily glued back on, or even, in emergency, sticky-taped. But he couldn't tell if there was further, less visible, damage.

He dreaded having to face the Leader, who still hadn't appeared. The MD sent members of the band out to search for her, while the producer made an announcement over the public address, explaining and apologising for the delay.

At length, the MD decided they would have to continue without the Leader. The other first violinist had never led anything bigger than a string quartet before. He settled himself uneasily into the leader's chair, adjusted the position of the music stand and asked for another oboe A.

The oboist tried to ease his obvious tension by some of the usual oboe replies, such as "What, *another* A, wouldn't you prefer the same A as before?" and "No, I've run out of A's today." He was too nervous to find these funny.

When at length satisfied, he nodded to the MD, who had long since had the "ready" signal from the stage. The first item, the opening song-and-chorus of the Second Act, was the very one marked by the beer-spilling and rosin-crunching incidents. He hoped the orchestra would let bygones be bygones and pull together. Indeed, this item went off uneventfully. In his relief, the new leader forgot to put on his mute for the next number, simply called "No.2, Song" in his part, but which he remembered was Yum-Yum's song 'The Sun Whose Rays.' Otherwise, the Act was proceeding competently, and the new leader began to relax, although he did notice the music was a little lifeless, he couldn't understand why.

Approaching the end of the opera, Katisha entered for her song 'Alone and yet alive.' Her costume included new jewellery with little mirrors, sending spots of reflected light into the pit, guaranteed to distract the musicians. He would have to say something to the leader. Ah, but he *was* the leader. So there really was more to being leader than just sitting at the front. As the MD conducted the start of her song, the new leader started to play his semiquavers and heard the source of the lifeless music.

It was himself.

He started to bow nearer the bridge, to project his sound better without playing louder, all the things he had noticed the Leader doing. He put in more expression, more vibrato, more phrasing, he breathed with the music, he started to transmit his *feeling* of the music more actively. Even though he could not get quite the same sound out of his violin as she did, the orchestra noticed his new tone and responded. Katisha at last had a worthy accompaniment, to which she did full justice.

A few bars further into the song, leading into the transition to 3/4 time, the double bass came in a beat early. Instantly, the new leader picked up his semiquavers at the new beat and led the rest of the orchestra by force of decisive example. He was however less successful in having his correct playing emulated in the next section, which was in the key of six flats, which every time had thrown much of this inexperienced orchestra into disarray, the note C♭ being especially hit-or-miss.

Shortly afterwards, as a matinée joke in the song 'Tit Willow,' somebody backstage sounded a bird-whistle throughout. Ko-Ko doubled up with surprise and could not continue, not that he could have been heard anyway through the audience's laughter. The MD stopped conducting. Immediately, against all his training, the new leader decided that he must ignore the MD because it would seem amateurish to have to re-start the performance – he must keep it going if at all possible.

Meanwhile the double bass had independently arrived at the same decision, and the two of them, though with mutes on as required in that number, insistently continued to pound out the accompaniment. The rest of the orchestra started to drift back in, and the MD started to speak Ko-Ko's words. Ko-Ko recovered his composure enough to resume, and the song ended as if this were all a normal part of the performance.

Soon, they had reached the end of the show. As the last of the audience were filing out, the real Leader appeared, having been able to enter the building as the departing crowd actuated the automatic doors. Her abject apology and explanation were interrupted by the other first violin showing her what had happened to her violin. As was correct etiquette when one's superior's instrument was disabled, he offered her the loan of his own violin for the evening.

She raged at him, "No! No! Do you realise you've smashed a Grancino? You careless idiot! No, I am not playing here this evening, how can I, you've smashed my violin! I'll sue you, I, I, boiling oil is too good for you, it should be melted lead! Oh, my violin!"

She then burst into tears, grabbed all her belongings and ran out.

The Jobsworth caretaker cheerfully announced that, under some obscure fire regulation which he had probably just invented, the auditorium would now be locked until the evening house. Musicians couldn't possibly use the rooms backstage, oh dear me no, but they could stay in the bar area – that was the licensee's responsibility, not his. Anyone leaving the building couldn't return until the automatic doors were switched to "admit" mode at 7pm.

The brass players headed off out, to the burger bar in the entertainments centre. The others, those who didn't have time to go home and come back, made themselves comfortable in the bar and unpacked their sandwiches and flasks.

"Looks like you'll be leading again, this evening," said the MD. "Even if I find another violinist who's free tonight, you know the production, you'll still lead."

"But you can't risk getting another violinist," the new acting leader pointed out. "What if the Leader turns up after all? Oh and by the way, can you have a word with the producer about Katisha's mirrors, they ..."

"I already did."

The new acting leader normally enjoyed this couple of hours' gossip and snacking between the matinée and evening performances. Not this time, with his worries about having to lead, the damage to that valuable violin, and the possible repercussions of the washing machine on his family life.

He went into the pit early and adjusted his seat and the music stand, assuming correctly that the Leader would not be there to share the stand. He made a great play of insisting on a proper tune-up, the one area where he felt the Leader had been lax.

As the auditorium filled, there was a sense of occasion. Someone said this performance had been sold out for weeks. The house lights dimmed and the MD entered under a follow-spot. He smiled at everybody, nodding to the new leader. The overture began cleanly, and the percussionist had long since overcome his early floundering at Bar 2, with a strong even beat. A few moments later in the overture, the viola had a solo quaver passage setting a new tempo, which had been shaky the first few evenings. The new leader looked round and smiled encouragingly at the viola. All went well.

The next danger point for orchestral ensemble was the three upquavers following the recitative 'Who are you who ask this question?' The new leader pinned his gaze on the second violin, who, for the first time that week, looked up sheepishly at this point, followed the MD's beat as re-inforced by the leader's gestures, and placed his notes in time, in octaves with the first violin. Phew, right at last, even if it was only for the very last performance.

But no time to relax. No.4, a men's trio, was sounding odd. The leader noticed the absence of the piccolo tune, which he was supposed to double an octave lower. It sounded to him as if he was playing in unison. He glanced across and saw he was. The first flautist, in her inexperience, had overlooked the change to piccolo for that number. Consequently, her tune, coming out an octave too low and the same as the first violin, could not be discerned through the harmony line from the second flute. The new leader transposed his own part up an octave at sight, to restore the tune to its rightful octave. Just enough notes of the introduction were left for the tune to become recognisable again and for the singers to find the pitch correctly.

His troubles were not over, not even in that song. Soon he was upon a set of awkward fast scale passages, which he had tended to leave to the Leader. His brain now in overdrive, he read all the accidentals and delivered a strong immaculate rendition.

While still wondering how leaders could keep up the concentration, he was being tested again, in no.5a, Ko-Ko's famous 'little list' song, where he had semiquaver passages all over the place with only occasional support from the flute and piccolo.

In the immediately following dialogue, Ko-Ko consults Poo-Bah in each of the latter's capacities in turn, dragging him from one side of the stage to the other as he does so. As this was earning good laughs, each night he would drag further, even down the steps that led down from the side of the stage, which happened to be where the percussionist sat. In order not to block the audience's view of the actors, the percussionist had taken to stepping off his stool during the applause at the end of the previous song and lying on the floor out of sight. The first violinists had noticed this but the MD never seemed to.

This evening, the new leader somehow guessed that the percussionist, after lying down, had completely dozed off. He alerted the MD, who passed a message down the wind players; the message reached the percussionist just in time for no.6, an unremitting grind of effectively dotted semiquaver rhythm for the leader, tonight solo. Against occasional competing plain semiquaver rhythms, he fought his way through the music. For reliability, he was using open strings where possible, but his A was going flat, and he couldn't disguise this as the second violin was playing in thirds with him. He had no spare moment anywhere in this song to tune it, but as he reached a page-turn, where he had to miss a couple of notes out anyway, he whipped his hand to the page and round to his string fine-tuner, which he gave a random twist. The gods were with him, it was exactly the correct adjustment to restore its pitch.

In the next recitative, the MD misjudged and conducted a chord change too early. The leader held his violin, scroll aloft, as a signal to the orchestra to ignore the wrong beat, and, good for them, they held off until *he* signalled them in. Good heavens, what had become of the disciplined obedient toady that he always used to be?

On reaching no.10, Nanki-Poo's duet with Yum-Yum, the MD remembered the difficulties this had caused at the band call. This made him waver slightly at the transition into 3/4 in the middle of the line "So in spite of all temptation ..."

With his new-found confidence, the leader took instant charge and, conducting with his scroll in his own tempo, played the introductory dotted quaver and semiquaver as if this were the greatest concert aria of all time. To his enormous satisfaction, the woodwind entered correctly at the start of the first 3/4 bar and all proceeded smoothly. The MD had the grace to smile as, for those few moments, he was not conducting the orchestra; in truth they were conducting him.

The leader was impressed with the potential of the young woodwind players, and just before the First Act Finale, whispered to the clarinets to make more of their rarely heard triplet figures. This was the catalyst to make the whole of this Finale, with its varieties of mood and orchestration, come into life as never before that week. The mood in the orchestral balcony in the interval was jubilant. He did not have the heart to tell these new players of the anti-climax that would grip them in a few hours, nor of how the tunes would go round and round their heads, until their next show.

He was now faced with playing the whole of Act Two as solo first violin, for the second time that day. Having done it once, and with everyone else thoroughly warmed up and on form, it was less taxing than he expected.

Just as he was relaxing, during a dance sequence, the draught from the chorus's swirling gowns caused the pages of the first-violin band part to flap over. When this had happened earlier in the week, he had resorted to leaning forward and pressing the scroll of his violin against the page. Sitting now at a different angle to the stand, he could not repeat this trick in time. He stopped playing and restored the page by a quick hand movement. He was alarmed how strange it all looked – he realised he had turned too many pages and turned one back.

But he was still not on the right page. In mounting panic, he flapped pages until he found the one that looked correct. He could not rely on the tune to jog his memory as to where he was on the page, because the tune was missing – it was him. Fortunately, the chorus was still dancing and the other musicians, especially the percussionist, were rallying round, adding extra interest to their parts to cover up for his silence.

Although this whole incident had taken only perhaps three seconds so far, his brain was buzzing with the dread that he would never now be asked to play violin in anything ever again, never mind first violin, let alone as leader. All these little things he would never see again, like the band part changing colour vividly from red to green, because of the on-stage lighting effects, every night at exactly the beginning of the second line.

At this precise instant, the stage lights changed from red to green. Could this be that very number? He played the first bar of the second line. It fitted, he was back on course. This must have been the longest four seconds of his life. Thank heavens for such an accurate lighting crew, he could breathe again. He even had the mental energy left to check the auditorium clock at the spoken words "The Mikado and his suite are approaching the city and will be here in ten minutes" and in due course was amused to see that, in fact, the Mikado arrived on stage in five.

There were speeches from the stage at the end of the performance, including fulsome praise for the orchestra. The MD gestured for them to stand. The leader waited a moment, before realising that the musicians were all watching him, to stand when he did, and to sit when he did.

He stood. The spotlight played around the pit and lingered on him. The applause was strong. He felt he had earned it. He had passed through a gateway and become a different person, a musically lonelier person. He was no longer a second violinist.

He decided to take the lonely country-lanes route home, over the hills. Under a bright moon, he saw rabbits and even a deer come out to watch his quiet progress. The excitement and glory over, it was time for reflection. Would he really be sued about the damage to the violin? Was it covered by his public liability insurance? He didn't know.

Then, he started to wonder what his wife would make of the washing-machine disaster and of his own inadequate response. Would she have gone to a launderette? Would she have left it all as she found it, everything sopping wet? Would this have been the final straw, what with all his evening absences, to make her walk out?

Which of their jointly treasured things would she have taken with her? What about his diary? My goodness, would she have taken the children too? All of them, or just some of them?

On reaching his house, he saw the lights still on. His youngest, who should have been in bed long ago, greeted him at the door. The child announced in excitement, "We've got a new auntie, she brought us a cake!"

The Leader had come round with the cake to apologise for her earlier outburst. Having helped mop up, she and the new leader's wife and the children were enjoying a lively impromptu party.

The Flautist

So it really was true. You could be chosen for your piccolo ability alone.

A well-regarded local reed player had phoned her with an odd request. He was doing *Kiss Me Kate,* in which, as was quite usual, he was required to play four different instruments. Would she do him a favour and come into the pit each evening to play just piccolo for him, and just the First Act Finale? In this number the piccolo, at the very top of its range, mimicks the heroine singing "never, never, never ...," and after a couple of nights he was finding he couldn't reach the top notes reliably. He had heard of her growing reputation, and perhaps she could help out.

She wasn't sure. She had just landed a busy and varied job which could involve evening overtime. She really shouldn't put this new job at risk, but, out of curiosity, she did finally agree to play. Within minutes of arriving in the pit, she wished she hadn't.

Were musicians all so bitchy? If she had known any of the people they were talking about, it would have been alarmingly informative, but luckily she would never know who it was, who was said to erase annotations before her dep played, so that the dep would appear to be accident-prone. Or who it was, who was said to have left her husband to sleep her way up the music education establishment. Or who it was, who ... The nastiest remarks were reserved for momentary human slips – miscounted rests, wrong accidentals, fluffed intonation – and came from players who were not necessarily themselves above reproach. Funny world this, down here in the pit.

And not just in the pit. A couple of nights later, up on stage, the scenery collapsed, a little before the scene in which the senator's private ambulance arrives noisily. By this time, she knew the show well enough to notice that the ambulance sound effect was starting far too early. She asked about it afterwards, and learned it had been a real ambulance, called to attend to an elderly gentleman in the audience who had fainted with fright at the scenery collapse.

She decided to disconnect socially and concentrate on her playing. Entering into the spirit of her one number, she had the boldness to go even for some notes higher than officially possible. Reassured by the laughter which her solo won every night (except VIP Night, when everyone was too strait-laced to dare smile, let alone laugh), she started to think she would rather like to play in theatres after all.

"Let *me* repair it!"

"You're a girl, you're our receptionist dogsbody, what can you know about PCs?"

"I'm fed up with being ignored. I like working here, this repair workshop's got a good reputation, but you don't know how I always had to finish my kid brother's models for him. Or all the other things I do. Like how I repair my flute."

"PCs are fiddly. Very delicate. Worth a lot."

"Look," she fumbled in her bag, "see these tweezers, see this jewellers' screw-driver for all the tiny grub screws. Oh, and look at these for hooking all those tiny springs in place. Now tell me that a great oaf-sized PC is delicate!"

"Oh, all right then, just because it's you. Piers, you show her."

The four young men in the partnership had to agree that she had made a neater job of the client's PC than they could have.

"OK, we've agreed to promote you. Stay late and do this overnight rush job for United Pharmaceuticals."

"Sorry, I'm playing in a theatre tonight."

It was the Friday of HMS *Pinafore*, only the second show she had ever been asked to do, and in fact the very first in which she had played flute as well as piccolo, but she was not going to tell them that. She was delighted to be doing it, but still felt as if on probation. In the fiercely competitive woodwind world, people were taken on one by one, selected only from the best, and then only occasionally. Even in very ordinary amateur orchestras, a flautist had to excel to be allowed even onto the waiting list, let alone get in, because lots of them were chasing a fixed number of places. Meanwhile, the number of places for string players was quite elastic.

Knowing that she therefore needed some edge over other flautists, she had decided that she could distinguish herself by extra care in intonation, and, after countless hours' practice, she could now pride herself on hitting every note spot-on. Even within each octave, every note required its own adjustment to the embouchure, blowing deeper into the lip plate if a flatter tone was wanted or to compensate for the relative sharpness brought on by louder playing; minuscule adjustments to her embouchure note by note, even for enharmonics. She was an expert at tiny adjustments to her stopper, moving it away from the mouth hole for pieces requiring low notes with good definition and power, or nearer where the upper octaves were more prominent, and in that case adjusting her playing accordingly to counteract the sharpness that would otherwise affect the higher notes.

It was this dedication to perfection that had originally made her learn the skills to repair her flute. Just before a recital, she had had to put her flute in for repair to a sticking lever. The shop lent her a fine-looking instrument, but her fingers skidded off its chromium keys, it had a closed G♯ key, its lip plate was the wrong shape, and everything about it felt strange and uncomfortable.

She was not going through all that again, she would learn to solder, tap, drill, ream, bush, temper, whatever it needed, to keep her own flute on the road. After all, she had half the skills already, from modelmaking.

At the beginning of the *Pinafore* week, she had wondered why she had ever thought she wanted to return to the theatre. All her big flute tunes were plonky and ordinary, and, worse, they were doubled by the clarinets or the violins. The dullness hardly made up for her few jolly moments on the piccolo. She also had a cold, which was bunging up her breathing. To cap it all, she was sitting right in front of the percussionist, who revelled in loudly practising his side-drum rolls.

Refreshingly, however, she felt she had moved from the cattiest pit to the funniest. In this pit, the players, all confident in their own ability, had no need to denigrate the others. They did make fun of each other – "Is that loud enough?" / "Oh yes, I can hear you clearly – in the General Pauses!" – but it was all in good humour. They all seemed determined to enjoy themselves for the week they were together. The string players in this band all seemed to know each other well, and talked and joked and played in the relaxed manner of a long-standing team.

Except that, to listen to them, nothing was ever right. Their violins seemed only to impede the sound they wanted to make. The strings were either old and dull, or new and harsh. The bow was either newly rehaired and not gripping properly, or due for a rehair and not gripping properly. The air was damp, the wood wasn't resonating properly. String players put themselves at the mercy of all this complex and outdated baroque-period technology to produce sound.

She, on the other hand, felt *she was* the sound. Her instrument made *her* sound for her. She had only to conceive the sound in her head for it to pour out into the hall.

After a couple of performances, she had identified the little snatches she could milk. She was learning she had some latitude, from noticing last night how the cellist had a few quavers introducing a slower tempo and change of mood in the hero's duet with the heroine in no.11. He milked these quavers shamelessly, revelling in how the singers would follow the tempo he had set, regardless of the tempo the MD was trying to impose. All right then, next night, she would show 'em.

It was a good night – the cello and bass had been held up by traffic and arrived too late for their pre-show drink. Their intonation was markedly better, at least until the interval.

She started with her 'icing-on-the-cake' snatch during the hero's tender soliloquy no.3, where the flute follows the clarinet (who played it straight) in representing a nightingale trilling. She couldn't alter the total time of her snatch, as that was fixed by a syncopated string motif, but she could push and pull within her allocated time. The flute might sound laid-back, but it required the same steady boldness that the piccolo did – every note could be heard through the orchestral texture – every note had to be right – every piece of phrasing had to be calculated. OK, she decided she would hesitate fractionally on the opening semiquavers, open the trill slowly, speed it subtly, hang back on the grace note, squeeze every last ounce of emotion from the moment, then fade on the closing quaver.

The trombonist leaned over and said, "Do that again and I'm yours for life."

Two bars later, without batting an eyelid, she did, even more meltingly. Why would the trombonist say that? He would never have said such a thing to a violinist, nor did he in fact say it to the clarinettist. It was because she was not just the player of the flute, she *was* the sound.

Except in no.7, where she had, not notes that were too high for the piccolo as in *Kiss Me Kate*, but notes that were *too low*. She checked, and yes, the part specifically demanded piccolo not flute.

Soon, the show had reached no.10, supposedly an

instructional song written for his sailors by the eccentric chief of the Navy. By this evening, she had got to know the song well enough not to have to painstakingly count off her 15-bar rests as the men sang unaccompanied – she knew now when to come in, and could meanwhile relax and listen to the words:

"His energetic fist" [on an impulse, she clenched her fist] "should be ready to resist" [she waved her fist] "a dictatorial word/ His nose should pant" [she wrinkled her nose, and her fellow musicians started to notice] "and his lip should curl" [she curled her lip], "His cheeks should flame" [she puffed her cheeks] "and his brow should furl" [she gave an exaggerated frown], "His bosom should heave ..."

The viola winked at her obnoxiously. To cover her perplexity, she gave especially sparkly treatment to the closing flourish of the number, a few bars of piccolo doubling violins in fast quavers. A moment later, she saw the leader's face appearing over the top of her music stand. He asked her to play the piccolo that way every night. It would add to the sound quality and would distract from the violinists' technical difficulties in that passage.

Shortly afterwards, at the same point each night, she became aware out of the corner of her eye of a child on stage (one of Sir Joseph Porter's sisters cousins and aunts) watching her intently. She found this very offputting, even more so after the clarinettist suggested it was probably a flute pupil. The trombonist, the viola player, now the child, she would really prefer less admiration not more.

In the First Act Finale, at the end of the chorus where the heroine plans to elope, she got the awkward sequence changes in fast quavers on the flute right for the first time. It was a symbolic success only, as these sequence changes were doubled by the clarinet, who seemed to have no trouble with them.

Then she had a short rest, in both meanings of the word, as the strings hold a chord, preparatory to Dick Deadeye's

entrance in which he halts the action by singing "Forbear ..."
[to elope]. The strings manfully held their chord with not a hint
of a waver, as seconds dragged into minutes as he failed to enter.
During this delay, she was amazed to hear musicians quietly
talking and giggling. How was this possible, talking while
playing? Ah, it was the string players! How unfair, string players
could giggle and still produce smooth unbroken sound.

At last, Dick Deadeye did enter hurriedly. She was glad not
to be playing herself, her breath would never have held through
all that wait, and she would probably have dissolved into
giggles too. At the interval, she said as much to the leader, who
seemed surprised but also pleased to be spoken to by her. She
seized the opportunity to enlighten herself on other queries:

"I don't understand all these words that get used. I mean,
what's the difference between a band and an orchestra?"

"Oh, some professor told me once, if it had violins, that
made it an orchestra. But I wouldn't worry about it."

"And what's the difference between a musical and an
operetta?"

"Ah, I'm not sure what it is officially, but I reckon it's got
operatic ambitions if it's got a viola in it."

She had so hoped her mother could come and hear her in
this pit, but her mother had no time to spare for her this week –
a new man had entered her life and she hoped they would be
moving in together soon. He too, her mother said, was
something to do with theatres and music, which decided the
flautist all the more strongly not ever to meet or accept him.

By the end of the week, she felt she was playing the piccolo
and flute as well as anyone could want. She was feeling better
than she had for days, noticing that her forced disciplined
breathing while playing had cleared her cold completely. She
revelled in the Saturday night applause – this was admiration
she *could* accept.

The next week started flat and empty, but she gradually

returned to her normal cheerful self, thanks to enjoying her work in the PC repair workshop and knowing she was seriously good at it.

She was lucky, as diligent people often are. Unknown to her, a visiting MD had attended *Pinafore* as audience and had become yet another of her admirers, in his case for musical reasons.

Just a week later, this MD, on being let down at the last minute by his usual flautist, sought her contact details from the Pinafore MD. And so came about her third show.

[continues after next chapter]

The Dep

She went home from her day job in a cold sweat of disappointment and impotent fury. She had been turned down for promotion because of her "lack of experience."

At least, nobody would question her experience this evening. She had deputised, she couldn't begin to remember how often, for ill or double-booked bass players in symphony concerts, chamber groups, cabarets, jazz gigs in pubs and clubs, everything. This time, she caught the call on her mobile, while waiting for the interview panel to announce its decision.

The caller was by day a cabinet-maker, famous in local musical circles for having made his own double bass, one of the finest in the county. That morning, he had chiselled into his finger. He was doing *Vagabond King* this week – could she dep for him tonight?

She was surprised and pleased he was still asking her. On her last job for him, *Oliver* a few months ago, she had propped her new mobile phone on her music stand. Although she had set it to 'silent ring,' she hadn't realised it would vibrate, rattling against the metal music stand before clattering to the floor. The MD was just then rising for the next number, and in twirling her bow into position, she had contrived to hit the percussionist's cymbal with it. This incident had somehow escalated until remarks flew and she found herself having to slap the trombonist. Either the whole story had never reached the regular bass's ears or he was desperate.

She used to resent never being booked in the first

place for any jobs, but was coming to accept her unique position as first emergency reserve for all the regular bass players. At least it saved her from having to attend band calls, which her friends confirmed seemed to take place on only the most glorious sunny Sunday afternoons; the more glorious the Sunday, the gloomier the theatre. If there was any disadvantage at all to her niche, it was maybe that the string players would be bound to be comparing her with the regular bassist, and she would never know how she herself came out of it.

She knew she was deluding herself really. Nobody paid any attention to the bass, nobody was aware of what you were playing, nobody noticed if you did a good job. The best way to tell was if the cellist strutted about proudly afterwards, as if he'd produced all the lower-string sound himself, then you knew.

She started to daydream through the many incidents that she had seen. There was that time in *Half a Sixpence* when the shop girls tell Anne of her boy friend's philandering. Anne responds by launching straight into her song 'I Don't Believe a Word of It!' Except, as she recalled in her daydream, the MD himself had been daydreaming. Within three notes, the whole band had come in before he had even risen to the rostrum.

Then the converse happened to her in *Gondoliers*, when the MD sat down prematurely at the end of a chorus and the band continued on, without conductor, until the end of the number.

Oh yes, that cold winter evening, when the guitarrist in *Annie* arrived in black motor-cycle leathers and didn't bother to change out of them, as it was an 'all-black' (not 'dinner jacket') pit. In one scene, Annie walks on with her newly acquired dog, which she has to convince a suspicious policeman is an obedient long-standing pet. On all the previous evenings, the dog growled angrily at the policeman, which was acceptably within character. But on this particular evening, the dog ignored the policeman. It was fascinated by the aroma of leather from the guitarrist and yapped excitedly, dragging Annie inexorably towards the pit, until two burly stage-hands came on-stage from the wings to rescue her.

Then there was that time when she arrived in the pit, found the ill player's bass in the pit and unpacked it. To her horror, his bow was German-pattern underhand. As a French-bow player herself, she had to spend the half-hour before curtain-up remembering from textbook pictures how to hold this German bow and then calling the player for final over-the-phone tuition, mobile phone in left hand and bow in right hand. Luckily, the show was *Mikado*, which she knew well, and by the end of the show, she was a convert to the German bow.

The theatres too varied so much. There was one where the flautist sat bent double under the cramped overhang of the stage, until he found a generous head-sized hole cut out of the ceiling, no doubt by one of his predecessors, where he could sit upright in more comfort. Then there was that theatre located within a pretty moat in a municipal park; the moat was home to a flock of ducks who decided to have a noisy squabble just as the heroine melted into the hero's arms.

One had a pit with the stage carried over it, at hardly above head height, on a system of pillars and demountable girders intruding into the pit. Her place was decorated with quilting crudely tied round a pillar and one of the girders. She wondered why, until her bow kept hitting the quilted pillar and, when she leaned forward to turn a page, the scroll of her bass crunched into the quilted girder.

She then recalled perhaps her worst pit, which was like

playing at the bottom of a mine shaft. She had been called to the matinée (only) of *42nd Street*, by a bass player for whom she'd never depped before. She didn't like his sense of humour, when he wouldn't tell her the time of the matinée, saying only "Chinese dentist, ha ha, get it?" She supposed it must be 2-30.

The pit was so deep and protected by tall guard-screens that the band couldn't be seen. The programme didn't mention the band at all, and she later heard that the audience thought the music was taped. She found she was the only woman, and incidentally the only string player, in the 12-piece band. In such bands, she would expect to be with percussion and trombones, but this time she found she had been placed on the reeds side, standing with a wall on her left and with the fourth reed on her right, as usual with scarcely enough room to bow properly.

The reeds' conversation was a revelation. They fussed about pads and levers and mouthpieces and gossiped about who had bought what in instrument sales, just like string players. The first reed boasted that he had found three packets of a long-discontinued make of irreplaceable rubbing papers in a closing-down sale. Instantly, the other reeds gathered round, insisting that he sell them at least a few papers each. This conversation reminded her to check in her pocket for her rosin, also a discontinued make and having to be used as sparingly as possible. She found, instead, that she had a champagne cork, given to each of the musicians as a good-luck gesture by the MD of *Pink Champagne* ages ago. She wondered why she had kept it all this time.

Circulating round the pit was a printed-out e-mail containing, as she gathered, a long complicated joke. When it reached her, she had to admit it was clever, but appallingly obscene. She smiled politely and passed it on. Obviously an induction test in this male environment.

The fifth reed was also a dep. The MD came over at the interval and praised him for the sonorous strength which he was bringing to the bass clarinet part, which in the double bass's opinion was actually mostly her own work, as the parts duplicated each other quite extensively.

Before she could become too worked up about it, one of the trumpets came up to see whether she was amplified, and, upon realising she wasn't, remarked admiringly, "My, you're putting your back into this!"

This, she reflected, was probably equally the good work of the fifth reed, so they were quits now, each being praised for the other's good sound.

The fourth reed, while playing clarinet, had his tenor saxophone ready on his lap. Unfortunately, an over-enthusiastic downbow on her part, with her new German bow with its long projecting button, smashed straight onto his mouthpiece and split his saxophone reed. He would be bound to say something to her, possibly even of an uncomplimentary nature, but for the moment she knew he would be too busy, fixing a new reed in place. Just as he was about to play on it, and too late for him to do anything about it, she had the inspiration of dropping her champagne cork into the bell of his saxophone. It was a tip she had heard some saxophonists talk of, to make the lower notes speak more easily, particularly in quiet playing. The cork was said to break up the heavy continuous column of air, and (so the superstition went) it had to be a champagne cork, as a wine cork wasn't big enough.

Almost as soon as he started to play, she could see a look of incredulous surprise on his face. The superstition was obviously reliable. With luck, his gratitude would outweigh his annoyance at the smashed reed.

42nd Street had a final surprise up its sleeve for her. In the closing number, a reprise of the title song, everything goes hushed as the hero ruminates on the beat of dancing feet that makes 42nd Street. At one point, his only accompaniment at all was her solo pizzicato.

Her daydream ran full circle to her interview failure, and she turned to concentrate on this evening, depping for the cabinet-maker.

She remembered the first time she had played his bass. She had attacked it like her own, expecting the same tired insipid tone. Out boomed a penetrating sonorous blast of sound. She looked forward to playing this fine bass again, and phoned him to check that it was at the theatre ready for her to use.

"No, you'll have to bring your own bass. I'm a sort of dep myself, I was going to cover from today to Saturday. No, I've not been to the theatre at all yet. Oh yes, thanks, it was only my third finger. I expect I'll have healed enough by tomorrow."

When she arrived at the city-centre theatre, she found the stage door flooded. She was directed up the fire escape, step by dizzying step up the external metal stairs slippery with rain, while gusts of wind caught her double bass threatening to topple her off-balance. At last, she reached the first floor doorway, which thank goodness had been propped open. Her relief was short-lived, as she found she had to make her way, bass slung over her shoulder, down a narrow concrete stairwell, bumping her bass on every corner.

Following hastily taped-up direction signs along this emergency route to the pit, she found herself in a passageway with big wicker baskets. As she passed, they rustled ominously. Mice? Rats even? On reaching the pit, she decided not to return to her car to collect her stool; standing for three hours was preferable to traversing that whole route twice more each way. Standing would also give her a better view of this exceptional Victorian auditorium.

At her music stand, she looked over the bass part. There was a typed list of cuts and changes, and her predecessor, or maybe it was the MD, had confirmed these on the part itself with yellow sticky notelets. The copyist had no faith in bass players; one number in A♭ had all the Ds printed with confirmatory flats. On the other hand, the part contained numerous mutes-on and mutes-off instructions, presupposing rather sensitive bass playing.

She was glad not to have brought her stool as there would have been no room for it anyway. The pit was unusually full; she counted two cellos, four violins, and something she had never seen in an amateur dramatic pit before, *two* violas.

On every chair in the pit was a programme. Not having a chair, she hadn't been given one. She took the programme off the seat jammed right in front of her: a keyboard, with a harp part on its stand.

That reminded her forcibly of her last show, *Carousel*, one night's depping a few weeks ago, where a keyboard synthesiser had also been used in place of a harp. There was a number near the end of *Carousel* where Billy had entered Heaven, and under his dialogue with a Heavenly Escort, the 'You'll Never Walk Alone' theme was quietly reprised. After a bar of solo "harp" in that *Carousel*, the strings had joined in to provide a more sustained harmonic wash.

A few bars later, the oboe had come in, quite sharp by comparison. The bass had stuck doggedly to her flatter harp-led intonation, thinking that to slide up to meet the oboe would sound ridiculous. She came to regret her decision, which had simply made the oboe sound ridiculous instead. She had meant to speak to the oboist afterwards to explain, but the oboist had gone before she had the chance.

Unbelievable. The oboist walking into this pit was the

same lady as in *Carousel*. Too awkward to put the bass down and walk through all the other players to talk to the oboist now. Never mind, perhaps at the interval.

The MD came quietly into the pit and looked anxiously at the still empty keyboard seat. On the stroke of curtain-up time, the keyboard player sauntered in. To make way for him to pass through, the string players had to shuffle around from their carefully positioned seating, causing one to kick over his open coffee flask. Players hastily picked their belongings up off the floor ahead of the tidal wave of brown liquid, and in the confusion the MD's stand was knocked over, tipping his score into the sodden carpet.

After all this, the *Vagabond King* overture was ragged and insecure. The dep bass player was however struck by an unexpected and rather good viola solo.

The bass player found she had an excellent view into the prompt-side wing from her position jammed up at the very end of the pit. She saw many little incidents to amuse her. An actor assisting another with a quick-change lost his wig and had to go on without it, lurking towards the back of a crowd until the wig could be passed to him by human chain. The prompt, who looked just like the prim librarian of *Music Man*, chased one character late for his entrance to push him on, and then ran back across the wing to gesture furiously to an on-stage character that he should be sitting not standing.

The actor playing the hated King Louis XI had an uncanny resemblance to Jigger in that *Carousel*. Jigger had brooding looks and self-assured sinister manner; Louis XI had all that plus understated menace and regal haughtiness.

The MD signalled the start of no.7 'Only a Rose.' The keyboard played an introductory harp cadenza, and then she with all the other strings joined in. A few bars later, in came the oboe with a solo, sharp by comparison. Oh dear, this was a rerun of that number in *Carousel*. It was a particular shame, as no.7 turned out to be a fine love duet, a hit known in its own right even outside the show.

The general lie of the bass part was very much in the lower register of the instrument, where sound production was sheer heavy work, doubly so for a standing player. She was finding it hard to hear whether her low notes were in tune, a particular problem when the orchestral tuning is ambiguous anyway. She was tiring and glad when the house lights came up at the end of the first Act for a short interval.

Carried away by reading her programme, having wanted to check whether Louis XI really was the same actor as Jigger, she realised she had left it rather late to have a conversation with the oboist. The bassist did catch up with the oboist in the backstage Ladies, but the oboist was at the head of the queue and talking intently to the flautist. The bassist thought she overheard the words "... he's walked out, thirty years ..." The bassist guessed this was no time to be making small talk with the oboist.

The orchestra tuned to the oboe for Act Two. Everyone seemed happy with the oboe A.

Though playing Act Two on autopilot in her tiredness, the bassist noticed that no.10c was titled 'Only a Rose – Reprise.' It had an even more impressive harp cadenza introduction than the original. Then the oboe entered, relatively sharp as before.

This time, the bass decided to take the initiative. She abandoned the harp's (keyboard's) intonation and slid her pitch upwards to meet the oboe. Thanks to the instinct of string players to tune to the bass, she was almost immediately rewarded by an extraordinary sound, like an ocean liner levitating, as all the other strings slid up in turn to match her.

When the remaining woodwind entered a few bars later, the tuning of the whole ensemble was sweet and together. The heroine at last had a coherent platform of sound on which to project her song. Suddenly the emotion became palpable. Ah, well, you couldn't beat these 1920s Viennese operettas for sheer romantic sentimentality. If the oboist was really having serious man trouble, she would surely be glad to come here into the pit to enjoy a few hours' escapism each night.

When the bassist next heard the keyboard player, which was not until the next Act, she noticed that his keyboard was now well in tune with the woodwind. So why wasn't it earlier? She wanted to ask him but decided it was none of her business. Anyway, her participation in the show, and with these players, would come to an end within the hour. She had the satisfaction of hearing the remaining numbers, even those with "harp", played and sung with a togetherness and enthusiasm rarely achieved as early in the week of a show as, in this case, the Wednesday.

"We strike at ten!" announced the Vagabond King. The double bass noted that the auditorium clock read 9.51. The King's men would have to move fast.

She could not quite follow who exactly were the goodies and who the baddies, or who was disguised as whom, or who was secretly in the pay of whom, but she realised the operetta must be reaching its end when she turned the page to see the Finale Ultimo, with just 'No.22 Incidental' immediately before it. She was too tired to notice that she should have removed her mute.

The tune of no.22 was one she had played many times this evening already. This time it sounded slightly different, and then she noticed it was strings-only. Meanwhile, something significant was happening on stage. Lady Katherine was stepping forward and saying something, she couldn't tell what through the music, but she had followed enough of the plot to tell that she was saving the life of the hero François, just moments before his execution.

Just ahead was a semibreve octave-chord E. On all the previous occurrences of this tune, she had gone for safety and played only the upper E, because the slightest error in intonation on such a low chord would make for a foul sound. In her surprise at Lady Katherine's unexpected move, she forgot and played the chord as written.

Instantly, a rich black velvet cloud of sound filled the theatre. The audience gasped, whether at her sound or at the dialogue she couldn't tell. The remaining strings, building on this wonderful foundation for their harmonies, added the fifth, the seventh, the tenth and further octaves of this enormously wide chord. François was reprieved and Katherine, whom he worshipped, would marry him. The operetta had been moving all evening towards this moment. The dep could not help feeling that Friml had written this musical climax especially for the bass.

The Finale and curtain calls passed in a whirl. The MD had concocted a playout long enough to empty the auditorium, but many of the audience stayed to hear it all and applauded at the end. She thought she had acquitted herself well, but knew nobody would ever tell her whether she had reached the standard of this week's other two bass players. She remained puzzled by the evening's intonation problems. One of life's insoluble little mysteries.

She noticed the keyboard player collecting the flautist on his way out. The flautist was exceptionally pretty, not to say outrageously glamorous, in the way of all flautists, but, oh dear, *he* was old enough to be her father.

The oboist was still there, slowly mopping out her

instrument. The dep decided there was no point opening a conversation with the oboist now; they might never meet again in their lives. She started to pack her bass.

The cellist, glowing with pleasure, said to her, "Been nice playing with you. This is a jolly good operetta, never noticed how good until this evening. And I felt on top form too."

The viola player whom she admired for that solo in the overture turned round and said, "That was much better tonight. Are you coming again tomorrow?"

The Flautist *(part 2)*

She had not visited the town since she was a girl. On her way to the theatre for the band call on the Sunday afternoon, she was driving round a bend and ... ah, oh, how wonderful, there, coming into view, was that monkey puzzle tree that she had so admired when she was small, still there after all these years, more magnificent than ever. Her heart rose.

The town centre had been rebuilt out of all recognition. Following her map, she found the theatre successfully but there was nowhere to stop or park, and she found herself sucked off into an expensive multi-storey car park. Once parked, she could not find the exit staircase to the street, ending up in an anonymous indoor shopping mall. It was as busy as on any weekday, but she had to ask several people before finding one who had heard of the theatre. And his directions were wrong. By the time she regained the open air, found the theatre street and arrived back at the theatre, she had only a short time to spare and was in a thoroughly bad temper.

Through the glass-panelled front doors, she could see activity in the theatre foyer, but all the doors were locked. Someone inside made pointing gestures, which seemed to be directing her to the side of the theatre. There, she found a narrow dank passageway, which eventually led through an emergency side door into the auditorium.

When her eyes grew accustomed to the darkness inside, she saw she was in a gem of a Victorian theatre. It was exceptionally lucky not to have been demolished by greedy councillors to make way for more shopping malls. The auditorium's colours, fabrics, plasterwork, delicately curved dress circle, chandeliers and ornate woodwork all contributed to a fairytale atmosphere. The auditorium had a couple of old-fashioned boxes each side of the stage. She had the vague recollection that she might once have been taken to a pantomime here.

She found her way into the foyer where she had seen activity and was surprised to see it set up for the band call. It was cramped and quite unsuitable, intersected by steps down to the front entrance and with brass handrails criss-crossing the space. Her stand had been set up by the front door, and she was now grateful to know that the door was locked.

"OK, everybody," said the MD, "glad to see you all. It seems we can't use the proper rehearsal room, so we're squeezed in here. The principals and chorus are coming later – they'll have to sing from those staircases up to the circle. Meanwhile," he continued, starting to hand out band parts from a pile, "I don't think you'll have any problems with the music. Oh, yes, for tuning, follow the keyboard, I've asked him to set it to 440 and lock it. Save you waiting for the oboe."

The string players jeered. They loathed playing with a keyboard. The flautist thought it was a particularly mutinous jeer, until she saw there were simply particularly numerous strings. This was an operetta, no doubt about it, it had *two* violas. One of them was the chap who had winked at her in *Pinafore*. She was more concerned to see as many as nine brass players as well.

As the band call proceeded, the flautist had to agree that the music posed no problems. It also offered no inspiration, though well enough written for the instrument. Already in the overture, she had a number of short solos. The music as a whole was dull and stodgy, heavily overbrassed, with a couple of indifferent tunes flogged over and over again. No wonder *Vagabond King* was hardly ever revived. The one amusing thing about the band call was the shoppers alighting from the bus stop directly outside the foyer and peering in, just inches from her face, to look for the source of the music they could hear. It was like playing to a street audience. Pity the bus brakes never squealed in tune. The idling of the bus engines provided a powerful pedal note, also not in tune.

The next night, the dress rehearsal, the flautist was relieved to see only four brass players. The rest had been deps, sitting in to prepare for their appearances later in the week.

There would be a delay in starting, as there was still a scaffolding tower in the pit for access to the stage lights. The flautist started to chat to the other musicians, and in a challenge as to who had had the fewest notes ever to play in a show, the flautist claimed victory. She recounted her *Kiss Me Kate* experiences, and, as her listeners accepted her and laughed with her, she began to feel like an old hand, even though this was only her third show.

When the pit was set up for the orchestra, the large number of musicians meant it was hopelessly cramped. There was the usual bleating from the string players, which she was learning was best ignored. The keyboard was shoe-horned in just behind her.

Somehow, the musicians accommodated themselves. Towards the end of the second Act, laughter returned to the pit as a quaver phrase in the Act Two Finale was erroneously played at 1-bar intervals around the pit – the orchestra decided it must be a fugue.

On Tuesday, opening night, just as she took off her coat in the pit, her mobile rang.

"Yes? Well I know my repair work's the best, it must be,

I've heard some clients asking for me specifically. You've had a meeting? You want me to become a partner? Well, sure, of course I understand it means we all take turns at the all-night rush jobs, and we all share the profits. Look, this is an awkward time, I can't talk now, the audience is starting to come in. Speak to you later."

In a muddle of indecision, she switched her mobile off. The one thing in favour was that the four computer men were such nerds that they hadn't the least interest in her as a woman.

In a few years' time, men's excessive interest in her would cease to be a problem. Oh, *she* would still be attractive all right – after all her mother was still obviously attractive thirty years older – but she would be quite safe in a pit or any other musical place; there would be no men left there. Boys had quite given up learning string instruments. Even double bass players were already mostly women.

Woodwind was now following this trend too. The few men who did play the flute were decent and often strikingly nice-looking, just the sort you would take home to meet mother. Except you couldn't, because they mostly ignored women. Meanwhile, the idea of being friends with, let alone marrying, a brass player was too outlandish to contemplate.

No more time for these reflections, the MD, looking magnificent in a tuxedo, was walking on, lit by a follow-spot. The production would now unfold to the public for the first time.

Already within the first few bars, she noticed she was essential, with little flute solos at several places in the overture including a particularly effective one at bar 20. Swap to the piccolo for no.2, sounded worryingly sour, but maybe this was just a passing intonation problem because of her two instruments being at different temperatures. With relief she returned to the flute for no.3 'Love for Sale.'

Intonation was slightly better, and she found she had another good solo early on in the number.

At the interval she switched on her mobile and, half-knowing it would be there, found a text message confirming the offer of a partnership. She was surprised how soon the end-of-interval bell rang, and then remembered from the dress rehearsal yesterday that this was a very short interval, with a second interval later. She hoped the second interval would be longer, although she didn't know how long to expect, as it had been taken up yesterday with the MD running a couple of numbers again with the orchestra and announcing some changes to the cuts, after she'd carefully marked them in with yellow sticky notes and paper-clips.

In the second interval, the other woodwind players took the flautist to the bar and, in doing so, discovered a short-cut, via the bar, from the street to the pit. The official stage door route was much longer. The shortest route of all would have been through the auditorium, but the theatre staff were exceptionally vigilant in not letting musicians go in that way.

Quietly, not to be overheard by audience in the bar, the flautist asked about the dire intonation.

"Oh, don't worry, it's opening night, it'll settle down. It's probably the strings."

This did not satisfy her. As an intonation perfectionist, she had even succeeded in accurately playing the hit song's awkward 'only-a-rose' ending semiquavers tag, which appears in successive octaves in successive bars, a flautist's nightmare.

On Wednesday, many roads in the area were flooded, which was possibly why the keyboard player had not shown up. Therefore, instead of tuning to the keyboard A=440, the orchestra waited for the oboe A, which she carefully checked with tuning fork before sounding it out properly.

When, in the nick of time, the keyboard player did arrive, there was some commotion as he made his way through the cramped pit to his seat, including the MD's stand being knocked over.

The overture was as bad as ever. Although the playing improved as the first Act unfolded, the oboe, to which everybody had tuned without complaint, still sounded persistently sharp. Puzzled, the flautist ran out after the oboist at the first interval. But the oboist spoke first:

"You play well, your intonation is sweet, you can tell me, what am I doing wrong? The orchestra tuned to *me* tonight and I was *still* wrong. Oh, never mind me. I can't think straight. He's walked out."

"Who has?"

"Thirteen years we've lived together and he walks out. He plays keyboard …"

"Well, you'll be glad to come into the pit and forget about it for a couple of hours."

"No, you don't understand, he's *this* keyboard player in *this* pit."

The conversation was suspended as they had now reached the front of the queue for the backstage Ladies.

In the next Act, in the middle of the reprise of the hit song 'Only a Rose,' for no reason that the flautist could identify, the intonation problems miraculously melted away. The singers responded, and the performance took off.

The flautist then idly glanced at the handbook dangling from the back of the synthesiser. It flopped open at the list of available instrument effects. She read:

0064 Harp Solo: faithful replication of the typical sound of a harp which has flattened unevenly in the warmth of a recital room. Note: Do not use 0064 with large ensembles; see 0065.

0065 Harp Tutti: harp sound with perfect intonation in equal temperament, suitable for orchestral use.

During the second interval, she craned round for a closer look at the synthesiser. A glowing display on the control panel showed **440:0064**. Applying an intuition derived from her day job, she pressed a button on the panel, and saw the display change to **440:0065**.

Many of the musicians were in the pit, eating ice creams bought over the pit rail, but she remembered the painful time her lip froze to the lip plate after an unwise ice cream, which had also deadened the inside of her mouth so she couldn't form a good embouchure. She skipped out to the bar in the hope of being in time to be served a drink. She needed one.

She would not get one. There was her mother with the keyboard player. What she hoped to avoid, their eyes met. Now she couldn't avoid speaking to her mother and her new man, at the end.

The remainder of the operetta was intense romance and high drama. The flautist was in the right state of mind to play accordingly. In this Act, *Vagabond King* offered her a raft of scary numbers in quick succession, no.12 'Tomorrow' in which she isn't called on to play until the last 27 bars, lots of triplets out of nowhere, difficult since she could never understand the intended mood of the piece. Then no.14c, an exit piece which is a naked unaccompanied flute solo with turns and downward octave leaps, no.15 with funny-seeming tricky fast jumpy quavers which she couldn't tell whether they were really meant as funny, or sentimental as in no.16 'Huguette Waltz,' a beautiful yet sinister number with difficult fast notes, at which she really felt she had excelled herself.

A moment later, a paper aeroplane hurtled steeply down into her lap. She looked up, and saw it had come from a young man, the sole occupant of one of the boxes overlooking the pit. What a sick prank. Then she noticed he was not a prankster but yet another admirer, for the paper aeroplane carried the message "I love you. I love your smile. Meet me afterwards." Silly young man, it was not a smile, it was an embouchure. Though she had to admit that, out of habit, she formed both facial expressions the same way. What if the message had missed and landed on the keyboard player immediately behind her, she wondered.

With the keyboard now set correctly, thanks entirely to herself for having read the handbook properly, she was gratified to hear how the intonation was now first-class throughout, even in "harp" passages. The strings were with her and the oboe now. The clarinets were watching their dynamics, carefully avoiding such loudness as would send them too flat. The singers responded with top-notch performances. The oboe solo in the third Entr'acte was stunning.

The performance was so successful that many audience stayed to hear the whole of the long playout, and applauded enthusiastically. The young man in the box was still gazing at the flautist. Fearing what he might have in mind, she gritted her teeth, ostentatiously took the arm of the keyboard player, and went out to meet her mother. What a miserable end to an unforgettably wonderful performance.

On the Thursday, the flautist expected an even better performance, but it didn't happen. Although she herself kept finding more and more passages, right from the overture onwards, where the flute or the piccolo made a real contribution to the musical effect, none of the remaining performances went as well as Wednesday's, she couldn't understand why.

Not that the Thursday performance lacked excitement. With the frequent changes between flute and piccolo, allowing the instruments to cool, she had good reason to fear condensation which could form a film of moisture especially over the tiny trill-key hole. Despite her constantly applying an edge of blotting paper under the pad of the key as a precaution, her piccolo was giving trouble which she couldn't explain, until she saw the pad itself was hanging loose, not clearing the hole even with the key depressed. Probably her own fault, when, in a hurry earlier, she had rasped the pad with a pipe cleaner.

Hoping that there was no smoke alarm nearby, she struck a match and let the flame play over the key. One of the violas gazed at her in astonishment – it made a welcome change from his normal ogling. As she had hoped, the heat softened the glue just enough to reseat the pad, at least temporarily.

Friday also had some excitement. To prevent the warmth of her lap from over-sharpening her piccolo, she had put it in her pocket. As she pulled it out for no.8, her first trill didn't. No time to worry, go for that above-stave B♭. Good. Now change to flute for the D, and now just 3½ bars to get the D above that! She managed to keep her nerve and hit the notes.

With a few moments to spare at the end of the number, she inspected her piccolo, to find a ball of fluff wedged under one of the keys. So much for storing piccolos in one's pocket for intonation's sake. She was wise enough not to use a pipe cleaner to shift the fluff.

At the end of the Saturday night performance, she looked at the pit, now knee-deep in paper petals strewn onto the stage in a woodland scene, empty ice-cream tubs, drinks cartons and chocolate wrappers. Not to mention a paper aeroplane love letter. What a sordid mess! Yet, what glorious music had been made here. And she had been picked to be part of it. Why should she give up the chance of more of these? One day, she would start her own PC workshop – she knew she was good enough – and she would *employ* people to do the evening rush jobs that would get in the way of her playing in pits. And if PCs were ever superseded, she could start a flute repair workshop. Come to think of it, why wait until then?

She switched on her mobile. "Piers? Your partnership offer, it's all very sweet of you, but ..."

The Percussionist

You never knew where they were going to put you in the pit. Usually it was on the MD's far right, behind the woodwind and brass. Very occasionally, if the pit was deep enough front to back, I'd be right in front of the MD. That made the most sense, because my rhythm, coming out of the centre of the pit, would unite the strings and wind *and* I could always read the MD's beat out of the corner of my eye without specifically looking at him.

But sometimes they'd put me behind the strings. Graveyard spot, unless you were lucky and the double bass was a rhythm merchant; you could have fun then. Otherwise, you see – string players are such a precious bunch – the only amusement there was to play louder and louder and see what the string players did. Putting on earplugs was one quite common response, or sometimes one of them would speak to me with elaborate apologies and hints, which of course I would fail to understand.

I mean, what else can you do but tease them? They ask for it. Just go into any bandroom and look. All the best settees are occupied, not with people, but with violin cases. So it leaves nowhere for anybody to sit, ridiculous.

I remember one *Guys and Dolls*, very unusual to have strings in that show at all, well, these string players, all of them were old dears in their sixties, very formal and polite even to each other, it was remarkable to see how they'd stay in the pit even during the interval, eating their high-fibre sandwiches out of waxed paper and twittering on about low-fat diets and Alexander Technique. They tried everything to quieten me down, until they hit on playing so quietly during the sentimental numbers that the MD told the rest of us, not only the brass but even the woodwind, to keep our volume down if we wanted him to book us again.

Well, he did book me again, to do *Annie Get Your Gun* early that autumn. Come the date, I was still on a disqualification for speeding, so I had to hire a van and driver, at Sunday rates too, to get my kit to the band call. We unloaded my stuff. For that show, it was timps, cymbals, bells, triangle, vibraphone *and* xylophone, traps and a Red-Indian type tomtom. I paid off the driver and got set up in the foyer for the band call.

We had a dreadful run-through. Half the orchestra were deps, with a couldn't-care-less attitude as they were going to do at most one or two performances. My band part was as unhelpful as I've ever seen, no song names on the part, not even any hint like 'Duet' or 'Chorus' or 'Utility,' no instructions on the part whether to use brushes or what, it would take me days to make notes for all the numbers.

The last straw was when the oaf of a theatre caretaker had some stupid reason why I couldn't leave my kit in the theatre overnight; I couldn't get a van, and no minicab wanted to know, so in the end I had to get a black cab. My kit wouldn't all go in, so my cabbie radioed for a second cab, and that's how I got home, in this expensive procession of two black cabs.

You can imagine I was in a bad mood when I turned up for the dress rehearsal, knowing how badly out of pocket I was going to be on this, my very first show of the season.

To cap it all, the MD tells me to set up my kit behind the strings. The pit was so tight my high-hats were going to be practically nibbling the cellist's ear. I was bound to get complaints from him.

But my position in the pit turned out well, I had a good view of the stage. There were places where the MD so misjudged the mood of the thing that I just had to take charge myself. It's not something to do very often, but when you do, the feeling of power is just total. You know the rest of the band will abandon the MD's stick and follow you, and you're holding the whole theatre in your hand; you're in absolute control of the emotional temperature. Those moments help to make it all worth while, but I tell you, don't go into music, it's too full of disappointments, just get a quiet office job. But back to that show.

For the rest of that week, I had to catch a suburban train to get to the theatre. I noticed there was a mile or two of old-fashioned clickety-click track just after Flockton, ending in a resounding *clatter, clonk* at Dell Junction. It drove me mad, how I couldn't stop myself counting the clickety-clicks as if they were bars' rests ... **133,** 2, 3, 4; **134,** 2, 3, 4; **135,** 2, 3, 4; *clatter, clonk;* drat, yesterday it was **136** before the clatter, clonk.

Anyway, this particular evening, I arrive in the theatre. The depping cellist finished yesterday, and now I'm waiting for the regular cellist to arrive, to see who he is and will it be fun to tease him, when in breezes this slip of a girl, swinging her white cello case as if it were a guitar. She was so cheerful and light-hearted, she never took anything too seriously. I began to find it was nice having her around, and I couldn't bring myself to annoy her with deliberately offensive drumming. It turned out she was the principal cellist in a film-studio orchestra – this was when film studios still had orchestras – and she was doing a bit of moonlighting for the sheer joy of getting some playing before a live audience.

Nothing fazed her. One evening, in the Sioux ceremony scene where Chief Sitting Bull adopts Annie Oakley into his tribe, the flares set off the theatre fire alarms and we all had to evacuate. The string players, except her, all went into a huddle whether to disobey the clear orders to leave everything behind, then got in everybody's way to fetch their instruments out with them.

Right odd they looked outside, dressed in pit black and clutching their violins in the open air. I'd have laughed if it had

173

been raining, they'd have gone frantic about their violins getting wet. Of course it was a false alarm, it was only the flares, but it made us twenty minutes late by the time the audience had all doddered back in. I missed the 22:38 and had to wait nearly an hour for the last train home. Well, I couldn't afford *another* taxi.

As the week went on, I did manage to write tips on my part to get a reasonably appropriate percussion tone colour for each number, no thanks to the arranger. Just as well too. When you were meant to hear Annie supposedly doing her new motorcycle stunt offstage, the sound effects people muffed it; on the spot I simulated a bike engine revving, by a timp roll during which I wobbled the tuning pedal to get a rise and fall in the pitch. Nobody said a word of thanks, though I saved the company from looking stupid.

As I got to know the show, I came to notice that the cello had a lyrical number at no.32, and very nicely she played it too, accompanying Frank Butler singing sentimentally about the sort of wedding he wants. Well, this particular evening, we were chugging through no.32 when I noticed something missing. Then I saw the cellist wasn't playing. Next, in a rest when I exchanged bell hammers for snare-drum brushes, I noticed she was holding the stand carrying my rack of drumsticks. I didn't have a chance to speak to her, because from then to the end it was all go on the bells, bass drum, snare drum and timps.

At the end of the number, she whispered that the locking pin holding up the stand had dropped out. She'd not only noticed, she'd had the presence of mind to hold the stand steady to save the awful noise of all my sticks and hammers and brushes crashing to the floor. And she'd foregone her showpiece number to save *me* from disaster. My heart really warmed to her.

From then, I positively looked forward to seeing her each day, until one evening she turned up in the pit in tears. She was always so open and straightforward, with such a zest for life, I couldn't think what her trouble might be. Eventually she calmed down, and I gathered her orchestra had been booked to do a prestige open-air fireworks concert the next summer. The guest conductor was going to put in his own brother as principal cellist, and she was to be demoted to second.

"What's the fuss?" I asked. "You'll still be at the front and the crowds will see you."

"Yes," she kept replying, "but it's going to include the William Tell Overture."

I gave up trying to reason with her. *Lone Ranger* music's the same as any other ...

"No," she wailed, "they know I'm useless, I was never really any good on the cello, they've seen through me at last, nobody wants me!"

"*I* want you!" I stuttered, before I could stop myself.

And it wasn't long afterwards she told me she was expecting my baby. So I had to let her move in with me. Her cat, that had caused rows between her and her landlady, it made itself at home, sleeping in my bass drum – it liked the blankets that were stuffed in the drum to muffle it. We did lots of shows together that winter and spring – it was one of the happiest times of my life. We made plans to get married as soon as possible after the baby was born.

She was able to wangle for me to play the timps in this open-air concert, as the programme had so many novelty numbers that it needed more percussionists than the film studio had on its regular payroll. Her pregnancy was going well, but I started to worry because the baby was due just a week after the concert.

I learned a lot at the rehearsal. *William Tell* begins with 47 bars of music I bet you've never noticed. My part started with 21 bars' rest, a *pianissimo* roll and 14 more bars' rest. If I'd not been listening out for what my girl was doing, I'd have said it would be more exciting to watch five archbishops playing bowls, but what's going on is a conversation for five solo cellos, and the principal has the juiciest of the solos. At last I could see why she was so upset at being bumped out of it.

My timp roll covers a bar which is silent for all cellos. As it fades away, she, on second cello, joins in with her very own solo tune. I vowed to myself that, in the concert, I would give her the most artistically sensitive timp roll in history.

The day of the concert was brilliantly sunny. We were to have a run-through that afternoon to check the technicals, you know, the open-air-stage arrangements, the mike settings and balance – all that sort of thing, and for the fireworks people to check the timings. It was relentlessly hot. Nobody could keep in tune. I didn't bother, because if I had screwed the timps up to pitch, as soon as it cooled down even a morsel, the skins would have stretched and suffered heaven knows what damage. But at least, stifling as it was, I was in shade. The cellos weren't. The principal's cello cracked under the baking sun and he had to sit it out in the shade of some trees in the park.

With the sub-principal viola having to lean over and sight-read the second cello part off the cello stand, my girl had to play the first cello part in the run-through. It was so beautiful we were in tears. So was she, of course. But soon, *William Tell* needs cymbals, and the junior percussionist picked up the pair. They looked to me old and heavy enough to have come out of the Ark, and Junior saw that the heat had finally pulverised their hand grips.

"Why you not play?" demanded the Italian guest conductor after the missing cymbal entry.

Junior eventually gave up trying to explain; the conductor's English wasn't up to it, and for sure our musical Italian didn't run to saying "the leather has perished."

At the end, the three percussionists, not counting me of course as I was down as a timpanist, argued about how they should place the tambourine, the castanets, the triangle, the block, the xylophone and heaven knows what else on the rickety table that had been provided at the back of the staging.

It was fun picnicking in the park before the public were allowed in. It was like my girl and I owned the stately home ourselves and the other cellists were our guests.

While we were changing into formal dress, in a pavilion reserved for the orchestra, the principal cellist made an announcement, in better English than his brother. The crack in his cello had spontaneously closed in the cool of the evening, and he would play as planned.

So my girl would have to play to my introductory timp roll without us having tried it out on that stage.

Musically, it was a brilliant concert. The cellos and violins were being eaten alive by midges attracted by the stage lights, except my girl was OK, she'd thought to lather herself with insect repellent. We weren't getting insects where we were at the back, but we were sweating hot under all those bright lights. My hands were so wet and slippery I could hardly hold my sticks.

We got to *William Tell*. While the compère was blethering on, Junior remembered where his spare pair of cymbals was, and just as the music started, **1**, 2, 3, he sidled past the table, **2**, 2, 3, he put out a hand **3,** 2, 3, to steady himself, **4,** 2, 3, lost his footing, **5,** 2, 3, lunged with his hand for a scaffolding rail, **6,** 2, 3, but his hands **7,** 2, 3, must have been as sweaty **8,** 2, 3, as mine, and he fell awkwardly **9,** 2, 3, onto the grass several feet below, he gestured in pain **10,** 2, 3, could I pick him up in time? **11,** 2, 3, I wondered, **12,** 2, 3, only nine bars to go **13,** 2, 3, before I'm in, **14,** 2, 3, and it's the one thing tonight **15,** 2, 3, that I can do directly for my girl, **16,** 2, 3, I don't think I can chance it **17,** 2, 3, to reach all the way down and pick Junior up **18,** 2, 3, no it's impossible now, **19,** 2, 3 concentrate on getting ready **20,** 2, 3, for the timp roll **21,** 2, 3, 1, 2 – softly but fast, bring it up, decrescendo, fade, in she comes with her searingly imploring melody, oh, it was all worth it.

OK, Junior, I've got 14 bars to lift you up now.

Junior was all right, got over the shock in a few moments, was right as rain for his cymbals entry. I can't remember much else until the concert ended. The fireworks started so suddenly, I'd forgotten to expect them, it put me right off my beat for a few bars, till we all got back into the swing of the piece. Couldn't see the fireworks of course, but I could tell what colour they were as they lit up the audience spread out all over the lawns. It looked magical. Well, so it should when you think what they charge the public. We got phenomenal applause and cheering at the end.

The timps belonged to the film studio, so I didn't have to bother about packing them away. I went straight to my girl, once I could drag her away from her fellow cellists, who were all hugging each other in delight.

"Aah!" she suddenly exclaimed in surprised pain. "It's coming! Hospital! At once!"

Boy, was I thankful for the private orchestra car park and the traffic staff who let orchestra cars out first. I drove to the hospital even faster than when I collected that old disqualification. The hospital admitted her at once and, it makes me sick to this day, that was the last I ever saw of her. She died in childbirth. Bet you thought that didn't happen any more. But it happened to her.

So we never did get married. But soon afterwards, I met Martha. She'd never worked in music and, to my relief, had nothing to do with music – you know what I think, it's too chancy a life and I wouldn't wish it on anybody. I was incredibly lucky, Martha married me and brought up the baby as her own.

I've never told you this before, because you were too young to understand, but you're a big boy now, it's your birthday tomorrow. You see, Martha isn't your mother at all, your real mother was that girl. Hush, William, don't cry, but I know it must be an awful shock. Listen, for your birthday, you've always wanted one and I've never let you have one, now you know why, but OK, we'll all three of us go out tomorrow and get you a cello.

The Viola Player

She had known what she was in for, when she took up the viola: the insults to the instrument and the bad jokes people loved to tell about it. She'd heard them all before, but still had to force a smile every time. Yet, unlike her subordinate role when she used to play second violin, she was often the lynchpin of the whole orchestra on the viola. Who filled in the vital third note of the triad in the closing chord? Who provided the momentum to keep the rhythm going in the second and third beats of the bar? They'd soon notice if every viola player went on strike one night, except they'd invent a viola joke round that too, no doubt.

She recalled that symphony orchestra rehearsal with that obnoxious conductor. "Come on, you lot in the gloombox department!" he'd snapped. "I don't tell viola jokes in this orchestra, I employ them!" To rub it in, he continued: "You remind me of the time when I was conducting a brilliant contemporary composition, brilliant it was, it included a passage where six violas make solo entries at semiquaver intervals. And do you know, the only way they got it right was when I told them to play it in unison."

It was quite unfair. Anyone who could cope with the extra weight and reach of the viola and master it sufficiently to conjure a good tone from it would find it easy to get a wonderful sound from any violin. Did these silly conductors have the slightest idea how difficult and fatiguing the viola was to play? Or of the constant attention a viola needed to keep it at its best, or how sensitive a viola was to the setup –

the position and fit and tightness of the soundpost, the shaping and position of the bridge, the make and age of the strings, the type of rosin, even the humidity..?

She returned to her present task of resetting her soundpost, which had somehow become dislodged. Should she put it just there, which accentuated the viola's characteristics of sombre darkness at the bottom, plummy richness in the middle and an almost human voice high up? Or should she move it along a bit, to damp down that variation of timbre with pitch? It really depended on which composer you were playing – some knew the viola and what tone colour they would get at what pitch and wrote accordingly; others didn't. Too bad if your next concert included works by both types of composer.

Her viola lying, so vulnerable, on her workbench looked to her like a baby. It almost *was* her baby. She continually fussed over it and looked after it. She knew its every line and curve and every feature of its woodgrain. She knew its moods, its likes and dislikes. She loved it. Despite all her ups and downs with the viola, how glad she was that she'd taken the plunge to learn it. She only wished she'd done it years earlier.

Her thoughts were interrupted by the phone ringing. In a moment she was shouting down the receiver, "Just leave me alone! How dare you call! I've got rid of you at last! We're divorced – or had you forgotten? You toad, you pig, you ..."

"No, wait, just listen. I hear you've become jolly good on the viola. Probably better than me now."

Incredulous, she could detect none of her ex-husband's usual sarcasm in his voice, but, if anything, a totally novel note of respect. She allowed him to continue. He was starting a week's run of *Calamity Jane* and had only just realised that it included a Saturday matinée, clashing with a wedding for which he'd long ago promised to play. Could she dep the matinée for him?

"No, but I'll do the wedding for you."

"Eh? I thought you liked doing shows?"

"Oh, come on! In a pit full of *your* friends?"

"So what's your problem? They won't laugh at you or anything."

"No, it'll be *you* that's the laughing stock, once they've heard me play and discover what a viola should sound like."

"Look, I'm double booked *this Saturday* and I can't sit around arguing for ever. You do the wedding, then. No, I don't know the happy couple, except they've had the good taste to want a string quartet; it was the leader who booked me. Oh, there's to be one read-through of the music beforehand at his house."

Warily, she asked who the leader was – he might be one of those who had been on her ex-husband's side during their split-up. But even as she asked the question, she suddenly realised she didn't mind any more. She was no longer afraid of him or his friends. She was sufficiently competent to meet any of his crowd on equal terms, and he had just admitted as much.

"I don't know any of you!" exclaimed the leader when the three other musicians making up the string quartet assembled at his house. It turned out that the leader's chosen second violinist and cellist, just like his viola player, had for various reasons been unable to oblige him, and the musical accompaniment for the wedding would now be provided by this crew of four mutual strangers.

The quartet was to play in the church before the service and during the signing of the register, and was then to play at the reception for long enough for the guests to come in from the receiving line and find their seats and settle down.

Operatic music had been requested, specifically melodies from some lesser known arias, and the leader had had to arrange these himself for string quartet. His arrangements turned out to be sympathetic and well suited for the four instrumentalists, except for the viola's concern about so many exposed open Cs. By the end of their rehearsal they thought they should succeed in making an adequate showing at the wedding.

One by one early on the Saturday afternoon, they arrived outside the church, an attractive building standing in the photogenic grounds of a stately home. The stately home had recently started to hire itself out as a wedding venue, and the reception was to be in one of the grand banqueting rooms of the house itself.

When the four had all arrived, with still an hour to spare before the wedding service, they walked into the church to set up. Their hearts sank when it became evident that there was no obvious place where they would have enough room to play. There was room by the altar, but they feared the more pious among the wedding guests might consider it sacrilegious if the quartet played there, especially as the music was secular. They bandied around various zany ideas, such as each of them sitting in a separate apse, until they decided to try moving one pew across the nave and the flower display with it, which would leave an adequate square area free for playing in.

The viola player and the second violinist staggered across the nave holding the flower stand as steadily as they could, until the viola player erupted into a fit of sneezing as the flowers stimulated her hayfever. The stand, together with the whole beautifully assembled flower display, would have collapsed to the floor had the leader not chanced to be near enough to catch it with a steadying hand.

Out of curiosity, the cellist climbed up into the pulpit, whereupon, when he could control his giggles, he pointed out that this new position of the flower display would obscure the preacher's view of most of the congregation, not to mention vice versa. So back the flower stand went, with the viola player standing on a pew, sneezing, to administer first aid to this now frayed flower display that must have taken enormous effort to assemble. Threading a stem here and patting a bloom into place there, she eventually restored the display to a presentable condition.

Now it was the leader's turn to complain. His bow would hit the flowers if they stayed there. He would move them. Profiting from the experience of the flower stand having nearly toppled over, he knelt down and eased the stand along the stone floor without lifting it. Growing bolder, he decided to move the flower stand as far out of the way as possible so that the four of them could safely shift one, or it might have to be two, pews to make themselves a space to play. Accordingly, he would temporarily move the flower stand into the pulpit itself.

Meanwhile, the cellist turned to the task of shifting the first pew. Finding it far too heavy to push or heave, he took out his cello spike and, using it as a lever, he knelt behind the far end of the pew and started to crowbar the pew across the aisle.

At this point, the bridegroom and his best man arrived in the church. Their first sight was of a viola player sneezing her head off and a violinist laughing fit to burst, as a pew inched its way across the aisle by invisible means, and a flower display made its way up the pulpit steps, also by invisible means.

The quartet-leader pulled himself together and outlined the quartet's playing-space requirements to the best man. He and the groom, who seemed quite pleased at the diversion, indicated where they had planned to be standing during the ceremony. With that sorted out, they lent their own muscle to the work of reorganising the church furniture, moving lecterns, pews and the flower display, until everyone was satisfied.

"Fancy being a churchwarden and setting the church up so carefully, and then having it all messed about like this!" exclaimed the viola player.

"Oh, this is nothing," the leader told her. "Church bell-ringers have always had an appalling reputation for, well, er, irreverence."

"You mean they drink and they swear," said the second violinist.

As the quartet were talking and joking, the first of the wedding guests began to arrive. The quartet thereupon settled in their chairs and tuned up. They played movements of their choice from books of Haydn and Mozart quartets, sight-reading some just for the challenge of it, finding to their pleasure that they were playing well as a quartet together.

Eventually, seeing the verger walking purposefully up the aisle towards them, the viola player enforced an exaggerated rallentando at the end of the section they happened to be playing, capped with a decisive *fah-mee* in the closing perfect cadence, to assure him they had now finished.

"The bride's arrived, and she's waiting outside the west door," he told them. "If you would please leave quietly by the south door, yes the side door, then she will enter, and you can follow her back in, yes through the main door, and sit at the back till you're needed."

The quartet did as they were bidden, and paid little attention to the wedding service, except to listen critically to the organist and spontaneously sing the hymns in four-part harmony.

When the bridal pair, followed by close family, went into the vestry to sign the register, the quartet padded forward into their playing positions and played the specially requested items. The atmosphere was good, and in her new-found confidence in the viola and in herself, the viola player even risked a few unconventional fingerings. And today, her fingers were magic: whatever she did, not a mistake did she make. Her viola was behaving too, her bottom C string staying rock-solid in tune. So it was for the others too, faultless playing as they breathed new life into what were frankly rather unprepossessing pieces of music.

They reached the end of the selection, but there was still no sign of the bridal party. As the four leaned forward to hold a *sotto voce* debate on what to play to fill more time, the verger appeared and whispered to them that the bridal party was about to emerge, and if the quartet would like to leave now, the organist would play some light piece to cover their departure, before the Wedding March. They eagerly agreed, as they had in fact been wondering how they were expected to be last out of the church, yet be set up and ready in the stately home before the guests arrived there.

They packed their instruments under the interested gaze of the congregation. They left the church and walked across the well-tended grass to the stately home. An attendant directed them in through the kitchen entrance, past crates of vegetables and carboys of cooking oil, along a maze of corridors into the reception room. Having set themselves up in leisurely fashion, they played another Mozart quartet for the pleasure of it, while they were waiting.

As still no guests had arrived at the reception – perhaps the photographer was taking longer than expected – the second violinist delved into his case and said apologetically, "I've arranged this fantasia on Bulgarian folk tunes for string quartet. Could you play it through to let me hear it please?"

"Well," laughed the cellist, leafing through his part, "I can play the first 167 bars all right," alluding to the 167 bars' rest with which his part began.

Guests were starting to filter in, but the quartet decided to try out this fantasia anyway. At length, after what seemed to be much more than 167 bars, the second violinist waved his bow to call a halt. All was explained. The cellist was not playing, nor was he counting, he was staring open-mouthed at the bride, locked into an expression combining shock, amazement and stupefaction.

The viola player, on this, her first chance to see the bride's face, recognised her as an up-and-coming singer of secondary operatic rôles such as Micaela in Carmen. And that explained what the arrangements were that they had been playing in the church – it was arrangements of her songs. It was she whose torrid affair with a cellist had been the talk of the semi-professional musical world.

Wait a minute – a cellist? No, it was a ridiculous thought. Surely not him. Yet, maybe …

Time for decisive action. It would be all the more effective, coming from a viola player. She took the gamble.

She thwacked the cellist with her bow, catching him square on the chin.

"Wake up, you chump!" she hissed at him. "We're playing the operatic selection again, and I mean now. Stuff your memories! Show 'em you're a professional."

The shock treatment worked. The quartet played as if inspired, the bass line and the inner parts all interweaving and blending with the melody into a magnificent rendition.

"Thanks," said the cellist at the end. Wistfully he added, "Don't really know why we ever split up."

They packed their instruments and left, this time arousing no interest from the guests, whose attention seemed to be elsewhere. As the four musicians made their way along the exit corridor, the viola player couldn't understand how such a brilliant performance could have elicited such a lack of response. On a hunch, she broke away from the other three and went back as far as the reception room door. She peered in through a glass panel in the door.

She saw the bride sobbing uncontrollably in her mother's arms.

The viola player hurried back out and caught up her three colleagues in the car park. There, the four of them decided to start meeting as a regular quartet and got out their diaries.